Delilah fought back the racking shudders that went through her...

Once she and Lucas had had to jump into a chopper basket before a bullet took them out. "Be careful," she whispered. "Your back—"

"Is fine," he answered. "You'll make it. I promise."

The thumping of the chopper blades drowned out Delilah's voice—and in seconds, the chopper came into view. She followed Lucas onto the open ice, praying they had time to get on board before anyone else could reach them.

"Go, go!" he yelled, pointing at the basket as it came down from the chopper. Lucas helped her in before hoisting his service dog, Haven, into it. The first bullet whizzed past Delilah's ear just as Lucas somersaulted in beside them. He motioned for the pilot to go, but more bullets came their way. "Stay down!" he yelled, covering Haven with his body.

They were going to ride this basket until they were clear of the gunfire, so all Delilah could do was hang on for dear life...

HOLIDAY UNDER WRAPS

KATIE METTNER

Harlequin

INTRIGUE

For the "Jameses" of the world. It takes someone special to do what you do. Thank you.

For the supply chain managers. You truly are unsung heroes.

Harlequin®
INTRIGUE™

Recycling programs for this product may not exist in your area.

ISBN-13: 978-1-335-45713-4

Holiday Under Wraps

Copyright © 2024 by Katie Mettner

Harlequin Enterprises ULC
22 Adelaide St. West, 41st Floor
Toronto, Ontario M5H 4E3, Canada
www.Harlequin.com

Printed in Lithuania

MIX
Paper | Supporting responsible forestry
FSC® C021394

Katie Mettner wears the title of "the only person to lose her leg after falling down the bunny hill" and loves decorating her prosthetic leg to fit the season. She lives in Northern Wisconsin with her own happily-ever-after and spends the day writing romantic stories with her sweet puppy by her side. Katie has an addiction to coffee and dachshunds and a lessening aversion to Pinterest—now that she's quit trying to make the things she pins.

Books by Katie Mettner

Harlequin Intrigue

Secure One

Going Rogue in Red Rye County
The Perfect Witness
The Red River Slayer
The Silent Setup
Holiday Under Wraps

Visit the Author Profile page at Harlequin.com.

CAST OF CHARACTERS

Delilah Hartman—As a former army cybersecurity officer, she knows something she shouldn't, and someone is willing to kill for it. This Christmas, she has no choice but to ask for help from the man she's been protecting for six years. He won't be happy to see her.

Lucas Porter—The former army warrant officer is now working as a security technician for Secure One with his PTSD service dog by his side. When he gets a call to pick up the ashes of the woman he once loved, he can't help but wonder what the real story is.

Haven—A former war dog turned PTSD service dog, he has one job—keep his handler calm and safe. He will go to any length to make that happen, even if it means getting in the line of fire.

Major George Burris—His side project put Delilah in danger. Will he go out on a limb for her now?

Secure One Crew—They've run a lot of missions, but going up against the people who trained them might be the one to bring them to their knees.

Chapter One

"Hey, there, Lilah," a voice said.

She smiled as she turned to him. "Luca. Where have you been?"

"Reloading our water and campfire supply. Did you find anything?"

"Sea glass," Delilah said, holding her hand out to show him a broken piece of pottery. It was worn smooth from tumbling around in the lake for years.

"Your favorite," he said, taking her hand and pulling her into a dance pose as he rocked her back and forth on the sand. "What will you do with all that sea glass, Lilah?"

"I don't know," she whispered, gazing into his eyes. "Maybe I'll make art from it to always remember the summer we turned twenty-eight."

"I hope you won't need the sea glass to remember." Luca lowered his magical lips to hers and kissed her like a man in love. While they had never said the words, they didn't need to. Their bodies did the talking. "I hope to be by your side the summer we turn sixty-eight." He spun her around in a wide arc until they toppled to the sand, where they stayed, laughing as Lake Superior lapped over them and the sun shone down to dry them.

"Luca, you're the kind of guy my daddy would have wanted me to bring home. I know it."

"You think so? I thought your daddy was strict about everything, including his little girl dating."

"Oh, he'd hate that I left the church and went to war, but he'd have loved you."

"Since he's been dead for twenty years, I guess I'll have to take your word for it."

"I've been thinking, Luca."

"Uh-oh. It's never good when a woman opens with that line."

Delilah rolled up onto her arm to look him in the eye. *"You won't think it's good, but I made a phone call yesterday while picking up groceries."*

"Who did you call?" His words dripped with defensive dread.

"The VA hospital in Minneapolis. It turns out they have a program there that helps veterans with PTSD."

"I don't need a shrink!" His growled exclamation should have made her pull back, but she was past that fear. Delilah knew he'd never hurt her, but he might hurt himself. She couldn't let that happen.

"It's not just a shrink, Luca. It's talking to other people in your situation and developing ways to channel your anxiety so you can live in the world as it is now."

"My PTSD isn't any worse than yours, Lilah." His words were soft this time, and he caressed her face as though she would drop the conversation and fall into bed with him. In the past, she might have, but with his episodes escalating, she couldn't put off the hard stuff any longer.

"But it is, Luca, and it's okay to admit that. We had

different experiences that did different things to our minds. I can't wake up to find you in the middle of Lake Superior again. Not when I know there are people who can help you."

"Will you go, too?"

"If you want me to," she agreed, even though it was a lie. "I'll do anything if it means you get help before it's too late."

"How long do I have to be there?"

"I can't answer that question, Luca. That's up to you and the doctors to decide, but from what I understand, it's usually one to three months."

He gathered handfuls of the warm September sand as he stared at the cloudless Wisconsin sky. "I don't want our time here to end, Lilah. When I'm here, I can forget what happened over there. When I'm holding you, I can forget about the men who—"

What was that music? It was familiar, and Delilah Hartman was supposed to remember what to do when she heard it. Her eyes popped open and she grabbed her glasses, slipping them on to stare at the phone screen.

You've been found.

Technically, that's not what the screen said, but she knew that's what it meant. Her gaze flicked to the time at the top of the phone. It was 2:37 a.m. Not a great time of day to tuck tail and run, but she didn't know if she had five minutes or five hours until someone started breaking down her door, so she couldn't worry about anything other than getting out undetected.

She slid out from under the covers and stayed low below the level of the windows. Her go bag was packed and easily accessible, something she made sure of every night before bed. Her only decision was how to exit the apartment. It was the start of December, cold, and the recent snow was going to make footprints easy to follow. She could walk out the front door as though everything was fine and it was any other early Wednesday morning, climb in her car and drive away, or opt for escape via the balcony. She'd rented this apartment for the balcony. Beyond it was a forest as far as the eye could see, giving her a place to disappear as soon as she made the tree line. This escape would be the eighth in six years. It was a habit she didn't like, and as she tied on a pair of boots, slid into her winter gear and slung the go bag around her shoulders, the truth settled low in her gut. She couldn't do this alone any longer, but the only man who could help her lived somewhere in the middle of northern Minnesota. The one thing she knew for sure was that she wasn't a Christmas present he'd be happy about unwrapping.

Then again, maybe he would be.

Delilah wondered how Lucas would feel about her popping back into his life unexpectedly after disappearing six years ago. He was probably angry that she'd dropped him off at the VA Medical Center and never returned. That wasn't by choice. If he wasn't angry with her, that would quickly change if she brought a passel of bad guys along with her, so she had to be thoughtful about her approach. None of that mattered if she didn't successfully escape from 679 North Bradley Street in one piece.

Her fingers found the scar on her chin and traced it while she rechecked the app. They had just broken the code and accessed her information, so there was no way they'd be here this quickly. She had time to walk down the stairs, get in her car and drive away. She'd abandon the car at the airport and hop on a plane. When she did, Lavena Hanson would cease to exist. The same way all those other names had over the years. Whether she liked it or not, it was time to be Delilah Hartman again if she ever wanted to live a normal life. Not that she could even define what a normal life was anymore. Normal ended the day she signed up for the army. What a lousy life decision that turned out to be. Not that she had many options. After her father died, her mother struggled to make ends meet, much less pay for college. Enlisting was a way to get her education paid for and come out with real-world work experience. Delilah couldn't argue with that. She'd gotten the necessary experience, but she couldn't use it if she wanted to stay alive. Not exactly what she'd had in mind as a fresh-faced army recruit.

Crouched low, she snuck out of the bedroom into the sparse main room of the apartment. The one-bedroom upper had been the perfect place for her when she'd found it nearly five months ago, but she knew better than to do anything but live in it like a hotel room. A stopover on the road of life. She'd been disappointed the first time she'd had to leave a place she'd made her home and promised herself she'd steer clear of using that word again. She patted the fridge on her way by, which held her only decorations for the holidays. Magnets in the shape of Christmas ornaments covered the front of it in holiday cheer. They'd remain there now for someone else to enjoy.

Delilah had her hand on the doorknob when she heard a commotion in the hallway. "Hey, man, you don't belong here," came her neighbor's muffled voice through the front door. She peered through the peephole, and her insides congealed with fear at the scene in the hallway. There was a man dressed in black with a gun, and behind him was the man who fueled her nightmares. He'd come again, and by the looks of the knife in his hand, he meant business this time.

She heard the *pop-pop* and was running for the balcony before she even registered that her neighbor had just been shot. *Don't die. Don't die.* She hummed to herself as she silently cut the screen and slithered down the rope tied to the balcony post for this very purpose. She hit the ground quietly, flipped her night vision goggles down, a throwback to her military days, and searched the grounds for signs of life.

Movement to her left caught her eye. The dude was in black head to toe but had his back to her as he faced the front of the building. Slowly, she turned her head to the right and saw another guy dressed the same at the opposite end of the building. Unfortunately, they were wearing night vision goggles, too, which meant she wasn't undetectable. She pulled her pistol from her holster and steeled herself. She had to make a run for it, but she had to do it right if she didn't want to be caught in the crossfire. She also didn't want more innocent people to die here tonight. Her bullets had to find their marks for multiple reasons, the least of which was this snow was going to make it easy to track her. Shooting on the run was always hard, but she had no choice. A part of her brain registered that this was the first time they'd sent more than two guys. Maybe that meant something, maybe it didn't, but she didn't have time to dwell on it if she wanted to stay alive. Her concentration could be nowhere but on getting to the trees.

A deep, steadying breath in and she ran, her movement catching their attention, as expected. The guy to her left turned first, and the pop of her gun had him on the ground before he got off a round. Unfortunately, the guy on her right heard the shot and swung his gun in an arc toward her. By the time his buddy hit the ground, she was already firing. Dude number two crumpled, and she turned tail, slid through the trees and ran like the hounds of hell were on her heels.

DEATH. NOT AN easy word to wrap a person's head around, especially when no one can escape it. At the same time, very few people live like they know that. Lucas Porter wasn't one of those people. He had intimate knowledge of how swiftly death came and held no illusions that he had any control over it. Lucas agreed with the idea that when it's your time, it's your time, but he didn't agree with the old saying that someone *cheated* death. No. No one ever *cheats* death. It simply wasn't their day to die. He'd seen it on the battlefield so many times. Days when three men rode side by side, an IED exploded and two died, but one was unscathed just inches away. That soldier didn't cheat death. He had something left to do before death took him. And it took everyone.

Lucas saw death enough times that he made the conscious decision to live every day like he was dying. He wasn't afraid of death, knowing it was inevitable, so he also made every effort not to leave anything unresolved in life. Unresolved situations only hurt the living, and Lucas never wanted to put that on anyone's shoulders. He carried some of those situations and feelings that could never be resolved as anyone does, but those memories were motivation not to create more.

He could accept those unresolved situations as casualties of the war he had been forced to fight. He went into the army thinking he could make a career, make a difference, right some wrongs—how wrong he'd been. He was sold a pack of lies, shipped off to a foreign land and given no choice but to fight for his life by taking someone else's way too many times. He understood it had to be done to protect his country, but he didn't have to like how it had to be done.

"Time to work, Haven," Lucas said, unsnapping the dog's seat belt from the SUV. "Get dressed." The German shepherd patiently waited while Lucas slipped the military-style harness over his head, fastened the buckles and then double-checked the patches to make sure they were easy to read. Six words stared back at him. PTSD Service Dog. Do Not Distract.

That was Haven's job. When they were at Secure One, the dog didn't need his harness to announce why he was there. He was an extension of Lucas, and everyone knew why. When on assignment, not a soul on the team cared about the real reason Haven stood beside Lucas. They knew he would defend any team member. Haven may have been the runt of the litter, but dressed in a black harness with his ears at attention, Lucas hadn't met anyone who would take him on.

Was he ashamed of having PTSD? No. He knew it wasn't his fault that he had it, but that didn't mean he liked announcing to the world why Haven was always with him. Despite the acceptance of PTSD throughout the country, it still carried a stigma that was difficult to see on public faces when they read the patches. He couldn't count the times he'd been told to "get over it," "just forget about it, you're home now," "just think happy thoughts" and "it will go away with time." Lucas wished even one of those things were true, but they weren't and it had taken a lot of therapy for him to trust in his coping mechanisms.

Truthfully, PTSD was a shared experience at Secure One, which Lucas had come to appreciate quickly. The team was great at pulling someone back who was falling too deeply into the past. Haven was trained to key in on Lucas and keep him steady, but he never ignored signs of anxiety from any team member. If they needed help returning to the present or decompressing from an assignment, Haven was there for them. He felt lucky that he could contribute to the team by sharing his dog that way.

"Today, you're all mine, buddy," he told the dog as he checked the SUV and glanced around the area, a habit he had picked up on the base that now came in handy working for Secure One. "If what Cal said is true, I'll need you to keep me steady."

A deep breath in and a walk up the sidewalk gave him time to focus on the perimeter of the past instead of the center of it. He reminded himself that he didn't have to think about his time over there, only the time he'd spent with Delilah on the beach six years ago. Determined to keep his breathing steady, he opened the double door and entered the funeral home. The plush carpet deadened the sound of his footsteps, as though even his footfalls were too loud for the dead.

Silence pervaded the funeral home, other than a piano rendition of "Silent Night" flowing through the speakers. Apparently, you couldn't escape Christmas music anywhere this time of year. A glance to his left revealed a small tree decorated with white lights, gold ribbon and a gold star. It was simple and understated, but felt like it belonged in the space where it sat. Recognition of the hope and peace of the season, even in a place where there was likely little of either to be found for families of lost loved ones.

He'd been told to ask for James, but first, he'd have to find a living soul in the building. Haven whined and stepped on Lucas's foot twice, a sign that his anxiety was building. He stopped and inhaled a breath, counted to three and let it out. Then he held his breath for the count of three, inhaled to the count of three and then held his breath to the count of three. He'd been taught several breathing techniques in therapy, but box breathing was the one that helped him the most. It distracted his mind and his body from the situation that was causing the anxiety. Technically, it was called the triple fours, but he'd modified it using a three count, something he'd been accustomed to using in the service and could do without thinking.

"Are you Lucas Porter?"

Lucas turned to a man dressed in a dark gray suit. His shirt was white, bright and starched, with a dark burgundy tie resting against his chest. He wore a name tag that said Edwards, Roberts and Thomas Funeral Home. James.

"I am," he answered, shaking the outstretched hand. "Nice to meet you, James."

"I'm sorry that it's under these circumstances."

Lucas suspected James said that a lot in his line of work. The man was shorter than Lucas's six feet, had a head full of blond curly hair and a baby face that was at odds with what he saw and did in a place like this.

"Me, too. It's been a long time since I've heard the name Delilah Hartman." That was a lie, for James's sake. Lucas heard that name every night in his dreams and thought of it every time he looked at Haven. "Is this situation common for you?"

"You mean having decedents arrive in the mail?" James asked, motioning him into a small room. At the front was a granite altar the size of a podium where an urn sat next to a spray of flowers. "More common than you might think. With the rise of cremation and the ability to send remains through the mail, we're often the go-between for families who live across the country to get a loved one home to a family plot."

"That makes sense, I guess," Lucas said, awkwardly shifting from foot to foot. "Not that I ever thought about it. We have a much different system in the military."

James patted his shoulder. "From what I understand, Delilah was no longer active military?"

"As of six years ago, she had been discharged. What happened after that, I can't say. I haven't seen or heard from her. That's why I was so surprised to get this call."

"I'm sure you were. I wish we could have softened the blow, but sometimes, there is no easy way to break the news to someone."

How well Lucas knew the truth of that statement. Too many times, he'd had to be the one to break the news to someone on the base that their buddy, girlfriend or boy-friend was not coming back.

"I understand that on a level that would probably sur-prise you."

James's gaze landed on Haven for a moment before he spoke. "Truthfully, not much surprises me anymore, Lucas. Did you serve with Delilah?"

"Indirectly," Lucas answered, inhaling a breath and holding it for the count of three. "Is that her?" He mo-tioned at the small altar where the urn sat. There was a laser-etched American flag on the front, the only indi-cation that the person inside had once served her coun-try on foreign soil.

"Yes. The box next to it is also for you. It came sealed and has remained sealed to maintain privacy."

"Do you know how she died?"

"I'm sorry, we don't. It all arrived in the mail with a note to ensure you got the items and Delilah's urn. We're still working to get a death certificate. The whole thing has also surprised us, but we'll try to sort it out. In the meantime, take as much time as you need. The room is yours for the day. Did you bring anyone with you?"

"Just Haven," Lucas answered, staring at the box by the altar.

"Then please, stay until you feel comfortable driving again. Would you or Haven like some water? We also have coffee and pastries."

"We're okay for now. Thank you, though."

"You betcha," James said with that classic Minnesota twang. "If you have questions, I'll be around. Don't think you're bothering me by asking them."

"Yes, sir," Lucas said with a nod. Haven stepped

down on his foot until Lucas shook his head. "Sorry. That urn is throwing me. Can we turn it so the flag isn't facing out?"

James patted Lucas's shoulder and walked to the altar, turning the urn until only the brushed steel faced them. "I'll be right outside this door." He showed Lucas where, and after he nodded, James walked through it and closed it behind him.

"Delilah, what happened?" he whispered, dropping Haven's lead and walking to the altar. He rested his hands on the cold granite and hung his head, the memories of the summer they spent together rolling through his mind and his heart. Those days had been some of the best and worst days of his life. While he hadn't talked to Delilah in years, he thought about that summer they spent together every one of the last 2,190 days apart.

Haven budged his leg with his nose, and Lucas snapped back to the room, eyeing the dog for a moment before he nodded and picked up the box. It was small and weighed almost nothing, which surprised him, though maybe it shouldn't. Delilah was never about material things. She was always about experiences. Probably because her job in the army focused on things. Things people needed and it was her job to get, and things that other people wanted and would do anything to obtain at any cost.

"Something feels smudgy about this, Haven," he whispered to the dog as he stared at the box. "Delilah was a veteran and would have been treated and buried as such, even if she had no one else."

Voicing what his brain had been saying freed him. He split open the tape on the box and moved aside the packing paper. At the bottom was an envelope that said Luca. She had always called him that, and he allowed it, but only from her. He recognized the slanting *L* immediately as her handwriting, so he gingerly lifted it from the box. Under it, taped to the bottom, was her army Distinguished Service Medal—the only possession she ever cared about in life and wanted to be buried with in death.

Chapter Two

Lucas pulled the medal from the box, tucked it into his shirt pocket and then slipped his finger under the lip of the envelope. He hesitated when he grasped the note inside. Hell, he did more than hesitate. His fingers shook, knowing that one of those situations he thought could never be resolved was about to be. He opened the note and stared at the handwriting scrawled across the page.

Hey, there,

Those two words brought everything back. Every touch. Every fear. Every moment they spent together seared his already muddled mind. The hope that the letter wasn't from her had ended when he read the greeting. That was their greeting. He always sang the words whenever he approached her from behind so she didn't get scared. He shook his head to clear it and forced himself to keep reading.

Don't show anyone this, Luca. I'm not dead, but I am in trouble, and you're the only one who can help me now. I saw in the papers that you're working for Secure One. They sound like great company

*to keep and just the kind of company I'm going to
need if you don't want this note to be my last will
and testament. Since I couldn't find their address,
I had to hope the funeral home could reach you.
I'm sending my medal along so you know it's really me. It's the only possession I care about other
than the one I left with you long ago. I need it back
now, or someone will make sure those ashes in that
urn aren't fake. I'll explain everything when you
catch up with me. I'm on island time now, but you
can call me at the number printed below. When
you come, come alone. Don't tell anyone. Don't
use the internet to search for me. They have eyes
everywhere.* Mele Kalikimaka. *Lilah*

Lucas lowered the paper to the table and stared at the
urn. What was going on? Was this a joke? He read the
note over and over until Haven whined and butted his
thigh with his nose. It broke his concentration, and he
glanced down at the dog, who put a paw on his leg. A sign
that his anxiety was too high. Lucas did another round of
breathing to calm his mind. When he finished, he reread
the note, this time with the trained eye of a security expert, not as a man who had once cared deeply about this
woman. Hell, as a man who still cared about this woman.

I'm on island time now. Mele Kalikimaka.

Why was she wishing him Merry Christmas in Ha-
waiian? The penny dropped, shooting Lucas to his feet.
"Boy, it's time to go."
He grabbed Haven's lead after folding the note and

tucking it into his wallet until he could return to Secure One. He was never more grateful that he'd be back on base in less than an hour, but first, he had to get out of there without raising any suspicion.

An idea came to him, and he pulled the medal from his pocket, rubbing his thumb across the gold eagle. Delilah always said after everything she did over there, the least they could do was give her a medal or two. She was kidding, of course, until she was notified that she'd be getting this one. The service had been short, but he remembered every second of it as though it were yesterday. He'd never been prouder of a human being than he was of her that day. Little did he know how quickly life would change right after.

Making a fist around the medal, he held it like a lifeline. A part of him couldn't deny that it was for the simple reason that, for the first time in too many years, he could feel Lilah in the present instead of the past. For now, he would play the part of a grieving friend, and while he knew too much about military funerals, he didn't know much about civilian ones. He stuck his head around the door and noticed James sitting at a table, working on a laptop.

The man lifted his head as though his tingly funeral senses told him someone was in need. "Everything okay?" James asked, standing and walking to the door.

"As okay as they can be when you lose a friend and fellow soldier." Lucas held out his palm. "She sent along her Distinguished Service Medal. It was the only thing she ever wanted buried with her."

"Was there a note indicating where she'd like to be buried?" James asked as they walked back into the room to face the urn. The urn Lucas now knew was, thankfully, not holding what was left of his friend.

"No, there was nothing else in the box. I know where Delilah would like to be spread, though. Am I allowed to take the urn?"

"Not yet," James answered immediately. "We're still trying to sort this out, so I can't turn it over to you until we have a death certificate in hand."

Lucas nodded solemnly, though he felt terrible that the funeral home was spending time and resources on a futile endeavor. Maybe he could fix that much, at least. "If you keep the urn, I'll move things up through the chain of command at Secure One and the military. Just sit tight and don't do any more work on it until I get back to you. There's no reason for you to dump a lot of time into it when I can get the answers much quicker and easier."

"Are you sure?" James seemed uncomfortable now, and Lucas wondered if he saw right through his words. "We're generally able to get all the information we need, but we're hitting a brick wall." So, he was uncomfortable because it looked unprofessional, not because he suspected Lucas was playing him.

"Likely because of who she was and what she did for the government. I can't say more than that, but I'm confident you understand what I'm saying." A curt nod from James was all he needed before he continued. "I appreciate the time you've put into this and for reaching out to us at Secure One. I'll find the answers you need and get back to you."

That was the truth. Lucas would get answers, hopefully, from Lilah herself.

"We're happy to help or facilitate anything we can,

once we know where to start," James said, walking along as Lucas moved toward the door with Haven following him dutifully. "Here's my card." He pulled a business card from his pocket and handed it to Lucas. "When you know something, please call. We'll go from there. Again, I'm sorry for your loss and that things are complicated."

"No need to apologize. Not when you did the hard work of tracking me down so my friend's wishes could be followed. I appreciate all your help. I'll contact you as soon as I know something."

With a final handshake, Lucas left Edwards, Roberts and Thomas Funeral Home and helped Haven into the SUV. As he pulled away from the curb, he glanced at the dog, who had settled on the seat, content that his handler was steady again. "Looks like we're going island hopping, buddy." Laughter filled the cab as he shook his head. "Too bad I'm going to need a parka instead of a bathing suit."

LUCAS WALKED INTO the cafeteria hoping to locate his boss. Whenever they weren't on assignment, the core team gathered for lunch to chat and plan for the afternoon. Today, he was both grateful and terrified that they were all there.

"Secure one, Lima," he said, releasing Haven from the lead.

"Secure two, Charlie," Cal answered, standing immediately and walking to him as a hush fell over the room. "Was it true?"

"No." The word expressed a heaviness he felt through his entire body. His feet felt like lead weights that tethered him to the ground. "It's a mess, though."

Cal held up a finger to him and turned his head. "Sadie, could you feed Haven for Lucas?"

"Oh, you know I will! Come on, boy," she called from the kitchen, giving him a whistle. "Time for lunch!"

Haven bounced on his front paws while he stared at his handler, awaiting a command. Lucas couldn't help but laugh before he pointed to the kitchen. "Rest time!"

The dog skittered off to get his lunch while Cal led him to the table to sit. Eric, Roman, Efren and Mack sat finishing their lunch. The same lunch magically appeared before Lucas as soon as he was settled. He pushed the plate away, his appetite long gone after the events at the funeral home. "Hey," he said, glancing around the table at the brotherhood he'd come to rely on over the last eighteen months. "I don't know where to start to sort out this mess."

"We're good at sorting out messes," Mina said, walking into the room with her noticeable baby bump. She was five months pregnant with a baby girl, and everyone at Secure One had pink fever. "Break it down for us." She sat next to her husband, Roman, who kissed her cheek as she got out her computer, something that rarely left her hands.

Lucas reached into his shirt pocket and pulled out Delilah's medal, lowering it to the table. It earned him four deeply inhaled breaths from the guys who had served in the army and knew it wasn't a medal just anyone received. "That medal is the only possession my friend Delilah ever wanted to be buried with her."

"This is the friend the funeral home called about?" Efren asked, eyeing the medal. "Not just anyone gets the Distinguished Service Medal."

"Yes, Delilah Hartman. We served on the same base. She was a security tech and supply chain manager. Since I was an ordnance officer, we interacted frequently. She earned that medal the hard way."

"Munitions," Roman said. "That's dangerous stuff."

"It is, but I was more on the IT side of the weapons systems. Since Lilah was also techie, we often helped each other with glitches in the field. As you know, the bases were well connected, but the tech was always at the mercy of what was flying overhead."

"Which made both of your jobs harder over there."

"It did on the satellite base. Oddly enough, our main base was in Germany, but we never ran into each other until we got on the smaller base. We had only been on that base for a month when it fell." Lucas cleared his throat and shook his head, trying to force the memories of that day down and away so he could focus on Delilah. Haven nudged his side, telling him he was back and ready to work. Lucas stroked his head several times as the dog put his paws on his lap. "We haven't seen each other in six years."

"Then, out of the blue, you get notice that she's dead and wants you to bury her?" Eric asked. "That's the military's job for veterans."

"It is," Lucas said with a nod. "That's why I was immediately suspicious. A box was sent with her remains. When I opened it, the medal was inside. I was with her when she got it, so I knew it was real. On top of the medal was a note."

"Read it," Cal said.

They all stared at him as he pulled the note from his wallet. He noticed his hand shook as he opened it. Was he afraid that, somehow, the words had changed, and she was dead? Truthfully? Yes.

"'Don't show anyone this, Luca. I'm not dead, but I am in trouble, and you're the only one who can help me.'" Lucas read the first line, and their brows all went up. "No one else ever called me Luca. I know she wrote this." Their nods told him they understood, so he finished reading the note to them.

Mina was already typing. "A 904 area code? Jacksonville doesn't make sense unless she's on Sanibel or Key West?"

Lucas shook his head and set the note down on the table. "It's not a phone number. Try 46.8135 north and 90.6913 west."

Mina typed and then glanced up at him. "Madeline Island?"

"Yep," Lucas agreed, his hand straying to Haven's head again. "After we were healed and discharged from the army, we met up unexpectedly in Duluth one night. We decided to camp on the island for the summer."

"'I'm on island time now,'" Roman repeated. "Smart."

"She knew if I got the letter, I would understand that she just transposed the numbers in the coordinates to confuse anyone else."

"What percentage of you believes she's really in trouble?" Cal asked.

Lucas reached for the medal, picked it up and ran his finger across the eagle again. "Every fiber of my being. I haven't heard from her in six years, and suddenly, out of the blue, she's sending me her ashes. No. For whatever reason, she's desperate. The way she mentions Secure One tells me that much."

"Let's talk about the elephant in the room," Efren said. "What do you have of hers that she wants back? It can't be the medal."

Lucas's fist closed around the metal eagle. "Oh, she'll want this back, but whatever she thinks I have, I don't have."

"I don't understand," Eric said, leaning forward on the table.

"I don't, either." Lucas's growl was enough for Haven to press his nose into his side again until he did his breathing while the team waited. They all understood how difficult it was when their service life crossed into their present life. "I don't have anything left from our time together. Listen, that summer we spent on Madeline Island was rough. We were both dealing with what happened on the base and its fallout. I'd been in a rehab facility for my back for almost two months and hadn't addressed anything that had happened to me, emotionally or physically. All these years later, I can admit that the PTSD was spiraling out of control, but she was the only one who could see it. Delilah dropped me off at the VA hospital in Minneapolis that September when we left the island. She promised to return the next day, but she never showed her face again. When I left the hospital almost three months later and started the training program with Haven, I tried to find her. By all accounts, Delilah Hartman had disappeared into thin air."

"We all know you have to go to her now," Mina said, typing on her computer. "Madeline Island is rather chilly in December, though. How long ago was this note written?"

"She's there," Lucas said with conviction. "Delilah

will stay on the island for as long as it takes me to find her, or until someone else finds her first. The box that her 'remains' came in," he said, using air quotes, "was dated less than a week ago from Minneapolis. That means she mailed them and went to the island."

"If she made it to the island," Roman said. Mina elbowed him, and he huffed. "Someone had to say it."

"No, you're right," Lucas agreed, shaking his head with frustration. "If she mailed the box from that far out, which I'm sure she did on purpose to confuse anyone looking for her, then she wasn't on the island yet. I still have to try. The fact that she reached out to me all these years later tells me she's desperate for whatever she thinks I have. Whether I have it or not is irrelevant. She needs help. That's something we can provide her, right?"

Cal was the first to stand up from the table. "No one left behind. This search and rescue will take some coordinating, though."

Efren stood and headed for the door. "Meet me in the conference room in ten minutes."

"Where are you going?" Cal asked, and Efren stopped in the doorway.

"If we're going to undertake a search and rescue, you'll need my future wife. Tango, out."

When Lucas turned back to the group, they were all grinning as they gathered their things. For the first time all day, he felt like he might be able to save the woman he hadn't stopped thinking about for six long years. If nothing else, bringing her back to Secure One and helping her out of this dilemma might be his one-way ticket to getting her out of his system. That, or finding her, only to lose her again, would make his soul bleed forever.

Chapter Three

Delilah crouched low in the darkness, praying the falling snow would hide her as she crossed the open expanse of the lake. She had lucked out. It was two weeks before Christmas and northern Wisconsin was in a deep freeze. That meant Lake Superior between Bayfield and Madeline Island was frozen, which didn't happen every year. The freeze allowed her to snowshoe to the island from the mainland under the shadows of darkness. She just had to be careful about where she stepped since there could be open spots she couldn't see in the dark.

She glanced down at her new white winter gear. Everything was new, from her snowsuit to her snowshoes to her backpack. Knowing she had no trackers on her didn't mean she was safe. It just meant it would take them longer to find her. And they would find her. Hopefully, it would take them even longer this far out from civilization.

Her choices were few, though. If the funeral home found Luca and gave him her "remains," she had to be on the island as promised. Were there better places to meet up with the man she'd abandoned without so much as a word? Yes, but Madeline Island would be a safe zone for Luca and his emotions. At least, she prayed it still would be. It had been enough years that she could no longer assume she knew anything about the man. She knew if he didn't show, she would have to initiate a more direct approach with him, putting both of them in undue danger.

Faking your death and sending an urn of fake ashes was dramatic, but Secure One was so off-the-grid that she couldn't find it. Considering all she needed was a computer for an hour and she could find anything, that spoke to the lengths Secure One went to remain incognito. Their business phone number was easy to find, but the address, not so much. They'd been in the news multiple times over the last few years, and Delilah had followed those cases, completely unaware that Luca was working for them. She was watching a news report on how Secure One had rescued two kidnapping victims from the Mafia, and when the news team panned out during a live report, Luca walked behind them. She had watched the clip at least two dozen times, trying to convince herself it wasn't him and trying to convince herself it was. Over the years, Delilah had kept track of him, but the last information she had put him as a guard for a state senator.

That was then, a time when she believed she'd finally outsmarted the people after her. But that time was over. Delilah glanced behind her, satisfied that the snow covered her tracks across the lake, even if it covered her head to toe, too. She had to get to base camp, set up her tent and get the stove going so she could dry out. After some tense moments searching for a way onto the island with thick enough ice to support her, Delilah finally stepped on shore. She'd made it. Before her stretched a winter wonderland that didn't hold the promise of snow-ball fights and cups of hot cocoa. It held the promise of death if Luca didn't find her.

He had seven days before she'd have to return to civi-lization or freeze to death. She didn't like either of those options, so she prayed Luca was willing to stick his neck out to find her despite breaking his trust years ago. She had to hope that his curiosity wouldn't let her down. He had always been a curious soul, and she had to play on that personality trait if she had any hope of convincing him to help. She just hoped popping back up in his life out of the blue would override the anger and disappoint-ment he surely felt about how things ended between them. Once they were face-to-face again, she could ex-plain why she ran.

A shudder went through Delilah, and it wasn't from the cold. It was from the memory that invaded her mind. She had dropped Luca at the hospital, her heart heavy as she pulled into the parking lot of her long-term-stay hotel. Barely out of the car, she was attacked by two men—one with a knife—and only managed to escape thanks to some kind older man who shouted out his win-dow when he heard the commotion. She'd been running ever since. She had reached the finish line, though. To say she was exhausted was an understatement. Nothing was left in the tank, and she feared what would come if she didn't get the only possible thing they could want.

Concentrate on the now, not the tomorrow.

Those were his words. He would recite them whenever she tried to talk about the future with him that summer on this island. Now, they were a reminder to take things one step at a time. Getting hung up on what could happen tomorrow manifested itself frequently and unexpectedly, but Delilah chalked that up to her PTSD. She had lied to Luca the day she told him she didn't qualify for treatment at the VA. She had simply convinced herself Luca needed help more than her. How wrong she'd been.

Those thoughts had to go back into the box she kept them in if she hoped to survive alone in the wilderness. She rolled her shoulders and stayed low as she approached the campground in case someone else was winter camping, too. She doubted it. As Christmas approached, most people were with their families inside a loving home filled with the scent of pine trees and cinnamon. She wasn't like most people. Never had been. All she wanted now was a place to rest—if not her tired mind, at least her exhausted body. Ironically, when she got the travel stove fired up to warm the tent, the scent of pine trees would be in the air. She would be thankful for that, too.

Campsite 61 came into sight, and she slowed as the memories rolled through her one after the other. Delilah lowered her pack to the ground at the ghostly sound of Luca laughing. Luca crying. Luca screaming in terror. The loudest of those ghostly sounds were of Luca loving her unlike anyone else ever had.

She lifted her face to send a message into the atmosphere. "Find me, Luca. I need you more than I ever have before."

When she lowered her head, she was sure of one thing: the countdown started now.

A WHISPER OF cold air swirled through Lucas, and he shuddered. It had been five days since Delilah mailed that urn, and he was running out of time to find her. If he missed her on the island tonight, he wouldn't give up. Those two words weren't in his vocabulary. Never give up, never give in. Those were the words he lived by. There had been plenty of times he could have given up, but there was an unseen force that kept him going. Death had walked alongside him, but he was still on this earth for a reason, whether he knew why yet or not. As he stared at the snowy tundra below, he was acutely aware of how unusual it was for the lake to be frozen this early in the season, so he couldn't help but wonder if this was the reason. If *Delilah* was the reason.

"You sure you want to do this alone, son?" Cal's words came over the headset he wore in the chopper as they flew toward their destination in Bayfield, Wisconsin. "I've been a ghost before. I can do it again."

"As much as I appreciate it, Cal, this bird is our ticket off that island, so I need you behind the controls. Delilah's note said to come alone. If I show up on the island and she gets a whiff that I'm not, she'll bolt. Besides, I don't know what I'm walking into. The less collateral damage, the better."

"That's the thing, kid," Roman said from where he sat next to Cal. "We'd be there to prevent the collateral damage. Think long and hard about this, Lucas. Having an unseen lookout may be the only reason you both walk out alive. You don't know why someone is after her, so for all you know, you're walking into a trap."

Lucas bit his lip as he considered what Roman had said. In the end, they were both right. It wasn't exactly smart to walk into the situation alone, but he also couldn't scare Lilah away.

"If we'd had more time to plan the mission, that would have helped," Cal said, as though driving home the point. "You barely let Selina call her contact at The Cliff Badgers Search and Rescue team to find the best way to get Haven to the island. I don't like leaping without looking."

"I know," Lucas said between clenched teeth as he stroked Haven's head. The dog sat beside him with one paw on his lap to keep him grounded. They'd worked together for so long now that Lucas never had to give the dog a command for help with anxiety. Haven knew it was coming long before he did. "I don't like it, either, but it's cold and she's probably been out there for days. If we wait too long, she'll dip and we'll be back to square one. We had to move on it and move on it in the dark."

Lucas waited, but neither of the men in the chopper said another word. Was he nervous about going out onto that island alone? Yes. But he was more nervous about seeing Lilah. He'd buried her so deep that he was afraid seeing her would dig up all those emotions he never wanted to see the light of day again. Did that make him a coward? Probably, but the truth was true, as his mom used to say.

"Let me ask you a question," he said, waiting for Cal to nod. "What would you do if you were me? Be honest."

"When I was your age, exactly what you're doing now," Cal admitted with a chuckle. "Since then, I've learned the importance of tactical strategy. I learned that strategy by almost dying more times than I want to admit."

"And he means that literally," Roman added. "I was there for several of them."

Cal reached over and punched his brother playfully while laughing. Roman and Cal were foster brothers who grew up together and joined the army. When they got injured on a mission and left the service, Cal went into private security while Roman went into the FBI. Now they were working together again, and Lucas trusted the two of them explicitly. The thought made his chest rise with surprise momentarily before he spoke.

"Are you guys familiar with the island?" Lucas asked, and they both made the so-so hand motion. "That's a no. Here's what you don't understand, guys. The island is much bigger and denser than it looks on a map. Lilah won't be near a paved road, so if you aren't standing next to me, you're impotent in an emergency. The forest is dense, which means the snow will hamper us even more. I know I need your help, but tactically, I'll be better off with you providing air support."

Lucas's mind entered planning mode. He ran through his intimate knowledge of the island, the best place to approach and all the ways he could stay hidden while doing it.

"It's impossible to be stealthy while offering air support," Cal finally said.

"That's fine, as long as you don't start this whirlybird until after I've met up with Delilah. I'll explain that I'm alone, but you're our ride out of there."

"You wear an earpiece and keep it on at all times?"

"All times?" Lucas shook his head. "No, I'll have to mute it when I approach her. I don't know what this is about, and until I do, I won't expose you guys to something that you can't deny to the authorities."

"You think it's that serious?"

"I don't know what to think," Lucas admitted. "I haven't seen her in six years, but the Delilah I used to know had never been dramatic a day in her life. She was calm, cool and calculated, so if she's scared and scattered, I'm terrified."

"Understood," Roman said.

"What's your plan?" Lucas asked, knowing they needed to be all on the same page.

"Don't you worry about what we're going to do, son," Roman answered. "Worry about what you have to do." He held up an earpiece for Lucas to see. "We'll all have one, and we can talk to each other." He held up his hand. "Yes, you can mute it so we can't hear you and Delilah talking."

"The rest of the time," Cal butted in, "mute is off so we can communicate. Understood?"

"Heard, understood and acknowledged," he said with a nod.

"Good, then let's get you out there to find this woman. My curiosity is piqued. I'm dying to know the story."

"Can we not use the phrase 'dying to know' for the next few hours?" Lucas asked, glancing out the chopper's window at the blackness below.

"Heard, understood and acknowledged," Cal said with a chuckle before he headed for solid ground.

Chapter Four

Lucas glanced at the sky as he and Haven stepped onto the island. The moon was starting to peek out from behind the clouds, which meant the temperature was about to drop again. He used hand motions to tell Haven to follow him into a wall of trees. When Lucas took the job with the senator as a security guard, he'd taught Haven hand signs he could use when situations didn't allow speech. The dog, a former K-9 in the army, had taken to the training immediately. Lucas had been grateful he'd already taught him the signs, so when he applied for the Secure One job, he could prove the dog wouldn't be a liability in a tense situation.

He paused for a moment and checked Haven over. The walk to the island had been less difficult than expected since the wind had blown them a path relatively free of snow. He'd come prepared with a sled at the recommendation of Selina's friend Kai, but it hadn't been necessary, so he abandoned it on shore for someone else to use. Now that they were on land, moving around would get more complicated. He straightened Haven's coat, checked his boots to ensure they were secure and did the same with his gear, including stowing his snowshoes on his pack. The shoes would only inhibit his ability to move quickly and efficiently through the forest and brush. If he was lucky, a path would already be made once he reached the campground.

Lucas clipped a short lead on Haven and quietly motioned him forward. They had purposely approached the island at an angle closest to the campground when he noticed a whisper of smoke through the trees as he stood on the shore. He had no doubt that the long-lost Delilah Hartman was awaiting his arrival. His mantra as he traversed the lake had been simple: *Stay neutral. Learn the facts. Act accordingly.* Something told him it would be a harder mantra to stick to once he was face-to-face with Lilah again.

"Secure one, Lima," he said into the earpiece.

"Secure two, Charlie," Cal said in his ear to tell him to go ahead and speak freely. If he ever heard a different greeting, it was an immediate signal that their teammate was in trouble.

"On the island, about half a klick from the campsite."

"Smoke in the air at your target. Proceed with caution."

"I noted that from shore. It's in the right vicinity for site 61. Will make contact in under five."

"The bird will be in the air in a few," Cal said, and Lucas could hear him flipping switches as they spoke. "I'll be waiting at the extraction point. You can hear us even if we can't hear you."

"You've got twenty minutes to convince her to leave with us, kid. Get it done," Roman said.

"Roger that," Lucas answered and then muted the microphone.

Did it annoy him that they always called him kid and son? It did initially, but now he saw it for what it was. Team members had to earn their stripes at Secure One. Until he did, he was a kid to them, but they never said it in a derogatory way. It came from a place of protection and teaching. Lucas had made sure to pay attention and learn those lessons well. If someone shared their knowledge with him, it only made sense to listen and learn so he could implement it when the time was right.

The time was finally right. He had no question in his mind as he silently approached the edge of the campground through the snow. Undoubtedly, Lilah was aware someone was nearby. That was who she was, but he couldn't worry about that as he approached. All he could do was continue to move forward, hoping she believed he'd come for her.

One last obstacle to overcome was the steep bank they had to climb. Lucas glanced at it and then at Haven, wondering if the dog could even make it, but the eye movement must have been enough because Haven plowed his way forward, forcing Lucas to follow as he held the lead. They were on top of the bank in just a few seconds. He was surprised how much easier it had been to scale that bank than it used to be. Whether that was due to the snow or the fact he took care of himself now was hard to say, but he was glad he was back on even ground.

Lucas stood in the tree line and took in campsite 61. A canvas cowboy range tent was set up with a stovepipe through the center, explaining the smoke's origin. The tent could belong to anyone. He eyed the area around it, noting a large wood berm built next to the tent the way they used to build their sandbag bunkers in the army. Lilah was here somewhere.

He had no choice but to announce his presence and wait. He unhooked Haven from the lead and pulled his Glock out from under his coat. After crouching into the shooter position, he flicked on his earpiece. "Found her campsite. I'm about to call out to her. Going dark for a few."

"Ten-four," Cal said. "Loop us back in as soon as you find her."

"Ten-four," he whispered, then put his microphone on mute.

Lucas cleared his throat and prayed his voice didn't sound like a scared twelve-year-old when he spoke. "Hey, there, Lilah." His words were firm but laced with the nervousness that filled him.

He'd been scared while running missions overseas, but hoping that Lilah was in that tent while worried she wasn't terrified him more than any of those missions had. He waited, the air crackling with tension, hope and fear. Had he missed her? Had it taken too long to get the message to him? Maybe she left information in the tent to tell him where to go next. Did he dare look? No, that didn't make sense. There was still smoke drifting from the stovepipe, which meant the fire was recent.

His gaze darted around the area, while his mind took him back to the time he had spent with Lilah here. It had been her suggestion to spend the summer on the island. After the base fell, they both ended up at the Minneapolis VA to heal, but never ran into each other. It was an unexpected meeting in a bar in Duluth that had reconnected them. That night, they'd shared a hotel room, not platonically, so he was all in when she suggested taking a summer to find themselves again before worrying about school or a job. They both had money; there was no problem in that respect, but they were both quick to realize they had no one but each other.

Lilah's parents were both dead by the time she was eighteen and Lucas never had parents to speak of. Sure, his mom was around, but she was too busy getting high to worry about what her kid was doing. By age eight, he was in foster care, so it made sense for him to join the service when he graduated. He had been led to believe it was his golden ticket in life after enduring a crappy childhood. Little did he know it would be a ticket to a house of horrors far worse than any childhood nightmare.

They'd brought only what they could carry onto the island, knowing there was access to everything else already there. That included access to nature therapy to help heal their fractured minds. Lucas glanced down at Haven and sighed. Nature therapy may have been enough for Lilah, but not for him. Still, all he could remember about his time at campsite 61 were the good memories—the memories of her touching him, loving him and protecting him from himself.

"Hey, there, Lilah," he said again, a bit louder, hoping she just hadn't heard him the first time. He doubted that was the case. Maybe she wasn't on the islan—

"Are you alone, Luca?"

The question came from his left, and he recognized the voice immediately. He fought back the wave of equal parts nostalgia and desire to focus on his pounding heart. *Stay neutral. Learn the facts. Act accordingly.* He ran the motto through his head before he answered.

"Other than my dog, yes." He had a decision to make. Keep his gun out in case she was being controlled by someone out to hurt them or put it away so he didn't scare her. "Are you alone?"

"I've never been more alone, Luca."

At the sound of her voice, he slipped his Glock into his coat pocket and stepped out of the woods with his hands up. "You're not alone, Lilah. You called, so I came."

And then, before his eyes appeared an apparition of his past. Delilah was dressed in white from head to toe. Even with most of her face covered, he knew it was her. The eyes never lied, and the gray ones hiding behind those prism lenses told him more than her words ever could. She had seen things over the last six years that haunted her and terrified her in equal measure.

Lilah pulled the balaclava down and sent him back to that summer under the Wisconsin sun. Life was complicated but simple. Love was in the air, and for the first time, Lucas was sure he'd found his family. He could still feel the softness of her skin under his hands as he ran them down her ribs to rest on her hips. Then she'd plaster her lips on his and carry him to another place where everything was simple. The only thing he needed back then was her.

Lucas hadn't agreed to get treatment for himself. He'd agreed to go for her so they could live the life they'd planned that summer. Once his treatment was over, they'd get a little apartment in Duluth and find work. They'd put down roots, learn about each other, build a life together, whatever that may look like as the months and years passed. He'd held on to that idea for the first month he was at the VA, hoping and praying that she hadn't visited because she was busy setting up their life. How naive he had been.

"I don't want you to leave," Lucas said, *holding her hand at the entrance to registration.*

"I don't want to leave, but you need to be here, Lucas. You must find a way to live with the horrors you saw over there. I don't want you to be a statistic. I want you in my life for years, okay?"

He trailed a finger down her cheek and tucked a piece of hair behind her ear. "You promise you'll visit?"

"As much as they'll let me," she whispered, *lifting herself on her tiptoes to kiss him. "In between those times, I'll find us a place and prepare it for your home-coming. I know we can do this if we do it together, Luca."*

"Together," he whispered.

Haven dug his nose into his thigh, leaned against him and rumbled a low growl as a reminder to return to the present. Lucas took a breath, his gloved hand stroking Haven's head as he gazed at the woman he'd been sure was lost to him forever.

"Delilah Hartman, long time no see." Lucas forced the words from his lips. His mind was having difficulty accepting that the woman who stood before him was the same woman he had shared so much with on this island.

He wanted to demand to know why she'd abandoned him. He also wanted to hug her and never let her go. She took a step toward him, and that was when he saw it. A scar ran from under the balaclava's edge to the side of her lip and another one across her chin and down her neck. The intensity of the situation was written on her face. The black bags under her eyes said she wasn't sleeping, and the fear in those globes of dusky gray told him she was scared, tired and unsure about everything. Everything but him.

"Luca. You came."

"Of course, I came. You fell off the face of the earth six years ago, and when you pop back up in my life, it's in an urn full of God knows what? I had to come."

"Sand."

"Sand?"

"That's what's in the urn. I'm sorry for the dramatics. I could find a phone number for Secure One, but no address."

"I'm just glad it wasn't you, Lilah." He took his glove off and traced the scar across her chin. "Help me understand. You dropped me off at the hospital and disappeared from my life. I waited for you for months, but you never returned. When I got out, there wasn't a trace of you. If you wanted to break things off, you should have at least said it to my face. I imagined all kinds of horrible things that may have happened to you."

"I know, I know." Her words were filled with desperation. "None of this was supposed to happen. I didn't want to break things off, but that choice was taken from me. You'll know everything soon, but we don't have much time. We have to get off the island. How did you get here?"

"I snowshoed from the mainland. How did you get here?"

"The same way. If we're going to get back before daylight, we have to go now."

She dashed into the tent, and when he pulled the side back, she was putting out the fire in the small travel stove. Once that was out, she grabbed her pack and flipped it over her shoulders.

"What's the dog's name?" she asked when leaving the tent.

"Haven." The dog immediately stood at attention next to his handler. "We went into a training program together when I left the VA hospital. He's a retired army K-9 turned trained PTSD dog. Haven is what allows me to function normally in the world we live in. He won't slow us down," he added, sure that was why she asked.

"That wasn't my concern," she assured him, holding her hand out for Haven to sniff. "If we're traveling together, he has to know I'm a friend and not a foe."

"Are you a friend, though?" he asked, the bitterness loud and clear in his words. "Or am I merely a matter of convenience for you?"

"No, Luca," she said, turning and stepping up to him so he had no choice but to meet her gaze. "I know you're hurt and you don't understand what happened. That's on me. I'll explain everything, but you're not a matter of convenience. You're the person I've been protecting all this time. I hoped it wouldn't come to this, but here we are, so first we must get somewhere safe, and then I can help you understand."

"I just don't know if I can trust you, Lilah."

"That's fair," she agreed with a nod of her head, but Lucas noticed her shoulders slump with shame. He instantly felt horrible. "I'll tell you how you can trust me." She pointed to the scars on her face and chin. "These are some of my visible scars from the last six years. There are more that damn near killed me, but they didn't—for one reason. I refused to die. If I did, they were going to come after you. Every scar on my body is a mark on the tally board of trust, Luca."

"How many scars are there?" His question was filled with anguish this time. The idea of her being tormented to protect him was too much to bear.

"We need to get out of here, Luca," Lilah whispered.

She wasn't going to answer him, leaving him with a decision. Do as she said and get them to safety so she could fill in the picture or press her here where danger lurked around any tree. Lucas held up his finger and flicked the mute button off his earpiece. "I need to let the team know we're on the move."

"Team? You said you came alone."

"I did, but two of the best army special ops police are in a chopper on the mainland. We were afraid to land on the island and draw attention, so I shoed in. We'll shoe back out and catch a ride to Secure One with Cal and Roman. You can trust them. I wouldn't be here if it weren't for them."

With her nod, he hit the button and spoke. "Secure one, Lima."

"Secure two, Charlie. Did you find her?"

"Affirmative," he answered, his gaze pinned to hers by an unseen force. "We're loading up and heading to you."

"ETA?" Roman asked.

Lucas did some calculating, considering that he would have to go at Lilah's pace and she was exhausted. "Haven will slow us down, so plan for seventy-five minutes."

"Ten-four. I'll have the blades going," Cal answered.

"Lima out," he said before clicking the mute button again.

"Haven will slow us down?" Lilah asked with her brow in the air. "You don't have to spare my feelings by lying to your team, Luca. I'm fully aware I'm a hot mess, but I want to get off this island alive, so set the pace. I'll keep up."

He should have known she would see right through his excuse, but being with Lilah again activated his protective side. There had never been a time since he first laid eyes on her that he didn't want to protect her. He would have died if it meant she lived, and he nearly did, but he forced his mind away from those thoughts. Concentrating on the past would do him no favors when trying to navigate the wildness of Lake Superior in the dark.

"We can't return to Secure One, Luca. We have to find the—"

The first pop confused him until a tree to his right exploded. Before he could react, Lilah grabbed his backpack and hauled him behind the wood berm, Haven hot on his heels. He dropped his pack and swung his automatic rifle to his shoulder, returning fire.

"What the hell have you gotten yourself involved in, Lilah?" His question was yelled over his shoulder as he tried to take out an unseen enemy. The question was rhetorical, but he swore he heard her say, "A living hell," right before the next barrage of bullets rained down.

Chapter Five

"They shouldn't be here already!" Delilah yelled as he ducked behind the wood. "I came in clean!"

"Someone forgot to tell them that!" he yelled as more wood exploded around them.

Luca had come for her, but Lilah couldn't help but think he'd brought some unwanted guests. Not that it was his fault. He couldn't have known that her every move was tracked by an unknown enemy. A bullet dug into the log fortress she'd built for this very reason. Haven pushed her back toward the woods, his experience with combat obvious as he protected her from harm. She was glad Lucas had Haven now.

There were a lot of cases of PTSD after the war. Hell, she had her own to deal with, but Luca's was by far the worst she'd ever seen. They had only been on the base a month when it came to an unexpected, barbaric end. She'd been protected from some of the horrors he'd seen, so she could only imagine what he'd witnessed before they jumped on that last Black Hawk out of hell.

Lilah noticed him touch his earpiece before he yelled. "Under fire! Need extraction! Need extraction!"

While he waited, he sent a few more bullets over the

top of the wood berm. If they didn't end this soon, even her wooden fortress wouldn't be enough to protect them.

"Negative," Lucas yelled just as more gunfire filled the air. He tucked his gun around the wood's edge and sent some bullets into the darkness. All Lilah could do was sit idly by and pray one of them would find their target. Her handgun would do no good in this firefight. "We're due east of Basswood Island. The airport is miles away!"

Lucas turned and addressed her as bullets slammed into the wood protecting them, throwing splinters into the air. "Who are these guys?" She saw him take notice of Haven, who had positioned his body to block her lower half.

"I wish I knew!"

Her words had barely died off when the report of gunfire ended. Lucas took his chance. He flipped his night vision goggles down, stood and sprayed the woods with bullets. He dropped down again and turned to her. "Two down," he said, and she wasn't sure if he was addressing her or the team in the chopper. "It seems like they'd send more than two guys." His gaze darted to her, and she shrugged.

"Hard to know," she whispered, in case others were out there. "I've always only been approached by two, but the last time there were four. This island is a bit of a needle in a haystack for two guys, so starting with the campground makes the most sense."

Lucas nodded and then spoke, but not to her. "The sat phone should have sent my coordinates." He stood cautiously, his gun aimed at the woods, as he scanned the area with his night vision goggles. "Still just the two," he said, talking to his team again. "Ope!" His rifle cracked once, and Lilah noticed a shudder go through him before he spoke. "Target down. Both targets are down." He nodded as he stood, searching the forest beyond the berm. "I don't see much choice. Yes, we can make it there in twenty minutes if we don't encounter more friends along the way." Lucas ducked back down and flipped his goggles up. "We have to move," he said to her. "Cal is bringing the chopper in to pick us up, but he can't risk landing on the ice. He'll get close, drop the basket and we'll have to climb in."

Knowing she had to help any way she could, she slung her pack off for a moment and dug in a side pocket, pulling out a handgun. "Don't ask me where I got it. Just tell me what to do."

Luca handed her a pair of night vision goggles. "Put these on and stay on your toes. The extraction point is two klicks west. We should be able to cover that in twenty minutes."

"As long as there aren't more guys waiting for us," she said, slinging her pack back on her shoulders.

"The only way out is forward," Luca said with half a lip tilt. "Haven, fall in," he said, and the dog stood and went to his handler.

"Side by side?" she asked, and he nodded once. "What about those two?" She motioned toward the forest.

"They started it?" he asked, and she heard all those same emotions in his voice that she'd heard when they were on the island so long ago. Disgust. Anger. Pain. Terror. Haven noticed, too, because he butted him with his nose three times. Luca stroked his head while he breathed in and out before he nodded. "Let's hope they're the last of it. We need to move. Cal is coming in over Big Bay for extraction."

"Ten-four," Lilah said but then held up her hand for him to pause. "Let's avoid the stairs. They could be waiting to ambush us there."

"Everything else is pretty craggy, Lilah," he said, grabbing her suit as she fixed her balaclava.

"Lucky for you, I already planned a route. You better let your team know it will only take us six minutes to get there."

"Six minutes?" he asked, dropping his hands. "That's impossible."

"Not if you trust me, Luca," she said, flipping her goggles down. "Follow me?"

Lilah stepped around the berm and prayed they were still alone and that he would trust her enough to get them to safety. Within a few steps, she heard them following and picked up her pace, jinking and jiving through the woods on a path she had memorized the first day she was here. It was one of several escape routes she had mastered because no matter what Luca thought, she would walk through fire to protect him.

"So far, so good," Luca said from behind her. "How much farther?"

"Two minutes," she answered, surprised by how easily Haven kept up with them as they ran. "I hear the chopper."

"They'll be waiting," he assured her as they ran, their heads on a swivel, waiting for a sneak attack that could end this reunion much quicker than she wanted.

As soon as the white ribbon came into sight, she threw her arm out as a sign to slow. "I marked this because the rocks here can have ice under the snow. You have to go slow, but you're also exposed, so stay vigilant."

Since she was the reason they were in this position to start with, she took the first step into the open so that Luca could follow safely in her footsteps. Funny. Up until now, they'd been equals in every way. Today, she could no longer say that about her relationship with Lucas Porter. While she'd been running for her life, he was building one. Suddenly, the wasted years without him weighed heavily on her shoulders. This situation was hers by default but not her fault. She just had to stay alive long enough to get that flash drive back from Luca and, hopefully, end this chess match for good.

Lucas and Haven met her on the ice, where she crouched low and waited. "Thirty seconds out," Luca whispered, and she nodded. "Roman will drop a basket big enough for all of us. Pile in and grab hold. Cal will take off while Roman lifts us on board."

"Ten-four," she said, fighting back the racking shudders that went through her. The scene felt too much like the last time they had to jump on a chopper and pray they made it inside before a bullet took them out. "Be careful," she whispered. "Your back."

"Is fine," he answered in her ear.

"It can't be like last time, Luca. It can't be," she said, the tone going higher with each word. "It can't be."

"Focus on three," he whispered into her ear. "Breathe in for three, hold it for three, breathe out for three. If you do that, you'll make it. I promise."

"You did always like the number three," she said with a lip tilt before she did what he'd instructed. The fact was, it did calm her and let her focus on what needed to be done to stay alive. "Maybe they only sent in the two guys."

The thumping of the chopper blades drowned out her

voice, and in seconds, it came into view. She followed Luca out into the open, praying they had time to get on board before anyone else could reach them. She wanted to believe only two guys were on the island, but she wasn't that naive. The two he took out were just their scout team, but the gunfire and chopper would now draw them like a moth to a flame.

"Go, go!" Luca yelled, pointing at the basket as it came down from the chopper. Lucas helped her in before hoisting Haven into it. The first bullet whizzed past her ear just as Luca somersaulted into the wire basket. He motioned with his arm over his head for Roman to go but quickly dropped it as more bullets came their way. "Stay down!" he yelled, covering Haven with his body while Roman returned fire.

They were going to ride this basket until they were clear of the gunfire, so all she could do was hang on for dear life and pray.

"THAT ONE GAINED purchase, eh?" Selina asked as she dropped a bullet into a pan next to him on the table. "Didn't anyone ever teach you to duck?"

Lucas meant to laugh, but it came out as a groan. "Must have been sick that day. Better me than Haven, though," he said, hissing when she stuck him with a needle and filled him with more Novocain.

"You're lucky you had that pack on your back or you'd be in a hospital. Maybe even a morgue."

"Trust me, I wish things had gone differently. We're lucky to have walked away with only minor injuries."

"Patch him up good, babe," Efren said, walking into the med bay. "They're not staying."

"They have to stay long enough for me to pump him

full of antibiotics and make sure this doesn't end up infected."

"Better talk to the boss about that. He says this is a pit stop to change tires and fuel up before they hit the track again."

Lucas glanced between them. "Cal wants us out?"

"He's waiting in the conference room to discuss it, but from what Delilah has said, if she's here, no one is safe."

"I haven't even had a chance to talk to her," Lucas said between gritted teeth as Selina started suturing the wound.

The ride back to Secure One had been short but tense. Lilah spent the ride holding pressure to his wound while all he wanted to do was hold her. Once they arrived at Secure One, Mina had whisked Lilah off while Selina tended to his leg. Thankfully, his pack had diverted the bullet and it lodged in the flesh of his thigh rather than his back or his head. In a few days, he'd be fine, but Lilah wouldn't be if Cal couldn't offer her protection.

Selina smoothed a clear bandage across the small wound, then snapped off her gloves. "That plastic coating is Tegaderm. You can shower with the stitches as long as the Tegaderm is in place. I'll give you some extra to take, but it's meant to stay on until it loosens itself. I used dissolvable stitches, so you don't have to worry about removal. They'll disappear on their own. Keep them dry."

"Thanks, Selina." He tried to stand, but she forced him back to the stretcher.

"Not so fast," she said, spinning her stool around. "You need antibiotics. If I can't give them to you via intravenous, then you'll have to take pills. We can't risk an infection. Especially if you won't be around for me to keep an eye on it."

Selina was their head medic on the team, but she was also an operative. In her prior life, she'd been a Chicago cop and search and rescue medic, so she understood the situations they often found themselves in when a case took a turn.

"Fine, give me the bottle." He held his hand out. "I need to get down to the conference room."

"I'll let them know you're on your way," Efren said before he kissed Selina on the cheek and left the room. It was only a few months ago that Selina spent her days snipping at Efren for every little thing. It turned out that forcing them together to save their own lives changed their relationship for the better. He could only be so lucky. Then again, the Delilah he picked up off that island wasn't the same Delilah he knew six years ago. She was different. Sadder. Untrusting. Harder.

"What's going on here, Lucas?" Selina asked, grabbing an empty bottle from her cabinet and counting pills from a different bottle.

"I wish I could answer that," he admitted. He climbed off the gurney, pulled up his pants and tested his leg. It was tender, but he'd had worse injuries in the field. "That's why I have to get down to the conference room. If Cal isn't going to let us stay here, I'll have to figure something else out."

"If Cal isn't going to let you stay here, then that woman is in serious trouble."

"And me by default."

"I also know that Cal isn't going to abandon you. He'll have a plan, so stay calm and listen to what he'll lay out. Twice a day for a week," she said, shaking the bottle before she handed it to him. "More a precaution than a certainty, but try."

"Got it, doc," he said, pocketing the bottle.

"Do you want me to keep Haven for you?" Selina asked, walking him and the dog to the door.

"Yes, but no. I don't want to put him in danger, but—"

"But you're going to need him," she finished, taking his hand to stop the patting to the count of three on Haven's head. "Before you leave, get his bulletproof vest. I know it's heavy, but it's smart to have the Kevlar on him in this situation."

"I agree. I should have done it when we went out there, but I wasn't expecting a full-blown war within minutes of arriving."

"I don't know anyone who would, Lucas. You got this. We're here for you, so if anything happens, you call in and we cover your back. In any way we need to, right?"

Lucas rubbed his hand down over his cargo pants, now torn from the bullet. "I feel terrible that Secure One has gotten hit with this after what happened with you and Vaccaro. I can't lose this job."

"Listen," Selina said, grasping his shoulder. It offered him a moment of solidarity in a situation he couldn't control. "You might be the newest member of Secure One, but you have saved all of our butts multiple times since joining the team. Cal knows that, and so does everyone else who will be around that table. Whatever is going on has nothing to do with you and everything to do with you, but not by your creation."

"Truer than you know," he agreed with a nod. "I'm afraid this will come to a fast end when I tell Delilah

I have nothing left from our time together. Then she'll disappear from my life forever, and I don't want that to happen. She may not be the Delilah I knew six years ago, but it's easy to see that's because of what she's lived through since we parted ways. If we force her out, I'm afraid she'll end up in an urn, for real this time."

"Then stand up and be the person she needs to help her out of this situation. We're here for backup, but we know you can do this."

"I'm glad someone has confidence in me. I barely got her off that island alive."

"But you did," she said with a wink. "You know what to do. You just have to remember how to do it."

Lucas stroked Haven's head three times and then met her gaze. "That's the problem. If I remember how to do it, I also remember everything else. Everything they taught me how to forget."

Selina leaned back on the wall and crossed her ankles. "Then the question you have to ask yourself is, if you don't help her, can you live with the consequences?"

That question had been sitting hard in his gut since they'd climbed aboard the chopper. He could give her what she came for if he had it and leave her to sort it out. But if he did that, would he be able to live with himself when she met an enemy she couldn't evade? The unequivocal answer to that was no. Knowing that he could have helped her but was too much of a coward would be worse than taking a stroll down memory lane. At least at the end of the walk, there was a chance for a happy ending.

Lucas kissed Selina on the cheek with a thank-you and left the med bay to rediscover his past.

Chapter Six

"I think this should fit," Mina said, handing Delilah a pair of black cargo pants. "They were mine before this." She patted her pregnant belly. "If they fit, I have several more pairs. You'll also need some of these." She handed her a stack of black T-shirts and sweatshirts.

"Black seems to be a theme here," Delilah said as she sat on the bed to pull on the pants.

"Makes it easy to match your clothes in the morning," Mina said with a wink before she handed her a pair of boots, also black. "Once we know the mission plan, we'll hook you up with the outerwear you need."

Delilah nodded but was only half-focused on the woman before her. The other half was focused on the man who had gone straight to the med bay to have a bullet dug out of his thigh.

"He's fine," Mina said, and Delilah glanced up. "Lucas. Selina messaged me she's already got the bullet out and the wound sutured."

"Luca took that bullet because of me. That's messed up."

"You weren't the one out there shooting up the island. Remember that."

"True, but I was the one who made a decision years ago that put him in danger. That was never my intention."

"I'm sure Lucas knows that, but you can tell him when we get to the conference room. Are you ready?"

Mina held the door for her, and then they walked down a hallway that could only be described as a fortress made of wood grain and steel. The log exterior made a person believe you were walking into a cozy log cabin, but instead, the interior housed high-tech security equipment and, from what she could gather, some rather deadly security techs.

The flight back from the island had been strained and nerve-racking. Cal was a master pilot, though, and managed to get them out of harm's way quickly. The problem? He made the point that whoever was after her now knew his chopper. Eventually, they'd show up at his door looking for her. That was not her goal. Her only goal was to get what she needed from Luca and go before anyone else got hurt. After he took a bullet on the way into the chopper, all she could do was hold pressure on it for the short ride back to Secure One. She hadn't seen him since. Delilah was desperate to tell him everything so he could promise to take care of her, but the chopper was not the time or the place. Instead, that time and place would be in front of people she didn't know.

Talking to Luca alone was preferable, but she also understood the complexities of the situation and that the team had to know the specifics. At least the specifics that she knew, which weren't many. She had suspicions, but that's all they were. She had no choice but to air her dirty laundry in front of all. Her steps faltered when she glanced up and noticed Luca walking toward them,

Haven by his side. "You're walking," she said when they neared.

"Of course," he said with a smile. "It was just a flesh wound. I suffered worse injuries on the base."

"I know, but that doesn't make me feel better. If you'd lost Haven or gotten hurt worse because of me, I couldn't go on."

"Good thing that didn't happen then. Now it's time we sort out who is after you and why."

"We?"

"We," he said, squeezing her hand. "Secure One isn't just a company. It's a family, and we take care of our own."

"I'm not one of you, though. My situation isn't your responsibility beyond giving me what I need."

"The moment you involved me in this, you became one of us. That's how it works, so there's no sense arguing with anyone here."

"Sounds like you already tried," Lilah said, holding his gaze. His brown eyes were just as bottomless as they had always been, but now they held a touch of something she couldn't name. Pain? Distrust? Or was it something else entirely?

Luca tipped his head in agreement. "They're already involved, so we may as well let them help us, right?"

With her nod, he motioned her forward into the conference room. There was a large whiteboard at the front of the room and a festively decorated Christmas tree in the corner that belied the reason they were here. A large wooden conference table sat to the left of the whiteboard with at least a dozen chairs around it. Filling those chairs were a few familiar faces and many unfamiliar ones, but they were all smiling as she walked in behind Luca and Haven.

"Welcome to Secure One, Delilah," Cal said. "I'm sure you're nervous after the situation on the island, but we're here to help, so don't feel bad about it. When one of ours is under attack, we all fight back."

"And make no mistake," Roman said, facing her. "You're one of us now."

"See?" Luca whispered in her ear, sending a shiver down her spine.

She might be one of them now, but in a few minutes, they would learn that what she brought to the table would take them back to the life they'd tried to leave behind.

"As some of you know, this is my friend Delilah Hartman. We were stationed together nine years ago in Germany before we were moved to a satellite base."

"What base?" Mack asked, taking notes on a pad.

"I wish we could tell you," Delilah said, biting her lower lip momentarily. "Unfortunately, we can't."

"You can't tell us the base you were on?" Efren asked to clarify. "What's the big secret?"

"The base," Lucas answered with a shrug. "It was classified. That's why you never heard about its fall. It was never in the news and was that way by design. I know you're all ex-military, so you'll understand that we still can't disclose the location."

Heads nodded around the table before Cal spoke. "Seems a moot point if the base no longer exists. We can work around it. Go on."

"Right, well, when we were discharged nearly eight years ago, we both had some recovering to do from injuries we sustained getting off the base. My back was broken in several places." He glanced at Lilah, who nodded. "Lilah suffered a TBI that left her with double vision, among other issues with her eyes." Everyone nodded, so he cleared his throat and went on. "When we were free of the hospitals, we ran into each other unexpectedly in Duluth. We decided we'd spend the summer on Madeline Island. The base fell in an unexpected and traumatic manner, but we had no time to decompress. We thought nature therapy might help as we considered our futures."

"It became obvious quickly," Delilah said, picking up the story, "that Luca—I'm sorry—Lucas started spiraling further and further into his episodes of PTSD. I knew we would never be able to have the life we wanted unless he got treatment as quickly as possible. While I witnessed atrocities on the base that day, they didn't hold a candle to what Lucas saw and did. I knew he would need a better way to deal with it before rejoining society."

"What Lilah's not saying is she saved my life several times that summer. She pulled me out of Lake Superior more than once," Lucas said, his spine stiff. Haven leaned into his leg, keeping him grounded in the room.

"Trust us," Mack said. "We've all been there. We understand the hard fight required to accept what we did when we had no other choice."

"It was one of those situations where I knew I needed help but didn't know how to ask for it," Lucas admitted. "Thankfully, Lilah realized it and got me into the VA hospital."

"While he was undergoing treatment, I planned to set up our new life in Duluth. That's when everything fell apart." She paused and shook her head as her gaze dropped to the floor. "I don't know how to explain what's happened since then."

"Just start at the beginning," Lucas said. "If we don't understand the beginning, we can't make this end."

"He's right," Cal agreed. "Feel free to use the white-board. Sometimes it helps to write things down chrono-logically for you and us."

Lilah walked to the board while Lucas took a seat next to Cal. He was just as anxious as the rest of them to find out what had kept her from him all these years. From the little she'd said and the scars she had, it wasn't simply because she didn't want to be with him. She had been fighting her own war these past six years. When she stepped away from the board, she had written and underlined several names.

"To start, you need to know my background," Lilah explained, pointing at the board. "I began as a supply chain manager for the army. Eventually, that morphed into cybersecurity, which is where I earned my keep. So, as a cybersecurity expert, it was my job to protect the base and to follow the intel on ops occurring off the base."

"Wait, you're a cybersecurity expert?" Cal asked, a brow raised.

"Well, I was six years ago. I may be a little rusty after being in hiding, but I've tried to keep my skills current. My commanding officer, Major Burris, knew I was also a supply chain manager. He ordered me to document historical antiquities found within the rubble and brought to the base by the locals or nervous cura-tors. The agreement was, once the antiquity, artifact or artwork was documented, I shipped it to a museum here in the States for safekeeping."

"Were you still doing that when the base fell?" Mina asked, typing on her computer.

"I was, but over the time I was there, I backed up all the antiquity information and shipping schedules to a flash drive," Lilah explained. "When I returned stateside, I learned that Major Burris was being investigated for war crimes. Something felt off, not that I could tell you what it was other than this feeling that I needed to protect myself."

"I think we all understand that feeling," Cal said. "We all did sketchy stuff on the orders of our commanding officers."

"Then you'll understand why I told no one I had the flash drive. I didn't want anyone to know until Major Burris's case had been sorted out. I worried that I may need it to prove my innocence."

"Rightly so," Roman said. "We all know bad things roll downhill."

Lilah pointed at him with a nod. "Exactly what I was afraid of, so I was happy to keep it under my hat and go on with my life. At least until I was either called to the stand or it no longer mattered."

"How many antiquities are we talking about here? A dozen?" Efren asked from his end of the table.

"Oh, times itself and then quadruple that, at least."

"Seriously?" Mina asked. "There were that many curators worried about their collection?"

"Considering how long the war had gone on, yeah. Think about what happened in World War II with priceless artwork. Mind you, they weren't bringing one or two things, either. They brought large collections of items they didn't want to fall into the wrong hands. Keeping track of it all and organizing the shipping schedule on these items was a full-time job that I was trying to do on the side."

"Did you get the Distinguished Service Medal for your work with the antiquities?" Eric asked. "That medal is only given to soldiers who do duty to the government under great responsibility."

"That defines what Lilah did over there." Lucas's voice held respect and adoration when he spoke. "If it hadn't been for her, no one would have gotten off that base alive."

"The medal wasn't for saving the antiquities but for saving lives?" Roman asked to clarify.

"No," Lilah answered. "The medal was for what happened when the base fell. I can't say more than that, but if you're implying that the antiquities cataloging wasn't on the up-and-up, you're wrong."

Roman held his hands up in front of him. "Not what I was implying. We're just trying to get a feel for what's happening right now, considering the situation on the island tonight."

"That's fair," she said with a tip of her head.

"From the news articles, Major Burris never went to trial," Mina said, her fingers stopping on the keyboard as she read the screen before her.

"I found that same information three years ago," Delilah agreed, stepping forward. "That's when I expected everything to die down so I could get my life back."

"That's not what happened?" Cal asked.

Lilah shook her head. "No, if anything, it got worse."

"What happened after you dropped me off at the hospital?" Lucas asked, his impatience loud and clear in the room. "You said someone attacked you?"

"Several someones. After I dropped you in Minneapolis, I went to a long-term-stay hotel. I planned to stay for a week so that I could visit you. I was barely out of my car when two men attacked me. I managed to get away when someone yelled out their window about the commotion, but not before they did this," she explained, motioning at her chin. "With my face bleeding and sliced open to the bone, I tore out of the city. The men who attacked me were trying to abduct me by knifepoint. I had originally thought it was a random attack until one of them said I should stop fighting and go with them because they'd keep coming until I gave up my information."

"Gave up your information?" Mina asked with a raised brow. "You were their information?"

"That's the vibe," she agreed, crossing her arms over her chest. "At first, I thought they knew I downloaded information before the base fell."

"Probably a time stamp in the code," Mina agreed.

"Right, that's what I thought, but then I realized that wasn't true. My flash drive has information that isn't downloaded. I transferred the information for each item to the flash drive before I put it through to shipping, so there was no way for them to know I made a backup."

"Which brings me back to the fact that at some point you were feeling sketchy about that whole side of the operation," Roman said.

Her shrug said more than her words. "As someone who works in the cyber world, I was protecting myself."

"Okay, so if that's the case, and there was no way for

them to know you made that copy, then they wanted you because you had the information in here?" Cal asked, tapping his temple.

"That's been my working theory thus far," she agreed.

"I still don't understand what I have to do with this," Lucas said, standing and walking to where she stood by the board. "I haven't seen or heard from you since that day at the VA. I have nothing left from our time together. What is it that you think I have?"

"The flash drive. I tucked it in your army bag for safekeeping."

Chapter Seven

Lucas took a step back as a shudder ran through him. "What now?"

Lilah refused to make eye contact with him when she spoke. "When we stopped at the storage facility in Superior before we left for the VA, I stuck the flash drive inside the bag so I didn't lose it. Since the storage unit was in both of our names, and I was going to set up house in Duluth, I had easy access to it should I need it while you were in the hospital."

"Why didn't you put it with your things?" Lucas asked, his teeth clenched tightly to keep from yelling. "You knew better than to ever touch that bag."

"I don't think that matters six years later, son," Cal said, trying to diffuse the situation. "What matters is now we know what Delilah needs."

"It does matter," Lucas answered, spinning on his heel. "I haven't opened that bag in seven years. It's a Pandora's box that would have grave consequences for me and all of you. It means reliving everything I've tried to forget. It means nightmares, flashbacks and losing the parts of me that I've found since that time."

"No," Delilah said, stepping up until they were chest-to-chest. "We aren't going to open the bag. The flash drive is in the outside pocket. I didn't open the bag, Luca. That's your history. I respect that. It was an afterthought on the way out. I had planned to move it as soon as I got back to set up the house. Somehow, we need to get to Superior and get the bag without being traced."

"No, we don't," Lucas said, gazing into her eyes. They were still terrified, but he noticed the same heat that was always there between them. Smoke tendrils that curled across her pupils to tease him into submission. "When I started working here, I moved everything in that storage unit to one just outside of town."

"Name?" Mina asked, already typing on her computer.

"Sal's Storage," Lucas answered without taking his eyes off Delilah. "Unit 57."

"That's twelve miles northwest of our location," she answered. "Corner unit with two doors."

Lucas heard them talking and making plans around him, but he couldn't drag his attention away from the woman who held him tightly in her aura. There had been an electric draw between them since the day they met on the base most unexpectedly.

The collision rattled his teeth. The cart in front of him had stopped dead in the middle of the road, and he'd had no time to react. When he looked up, a woman was on the ground next to the cart. Lucas jumped out, running to the woman staring at the blue sky, blinking every few seconds.

"Are you okay?" Lucas asked, checking her over for injuries. "I didn't have time to react, much less stop."

The woman blinked twice more, drawing his eye to hers. They were the most unusual shade of gray but

*beautifully framed by her heart-shaped face. Her straw-
berry blond hair was shoulder-length and topped with
an army cap. She let out a puff of air, and he couldn't
help but smile at the way her Cupid's bow lips puckered
as she tried to form words.*

*"I'm fine," she finally managed to say. "Just stunned.
Help me up."*

*"Maybe we should call for help first? Make sure you
don't have anything wrong with your head or neck?"*

*"I don't," she promised, pushing herself to a sitting
position. "Just got the wind knocked out of me when
we collided."*

*"I'm Lucas," he said, sticking his hand out to help
her. "Glad you're okay."*

*"Thanks," she said, taking his hand until she was
upright. She seemed hesitant to drop it, so he didn't let
her. He held it loosely while they stood on the old tarmac. "I don't know what happened, but it just came to
a grinding halt and tossed me out."*

*Lucas released her hand and crouched to look under
the cart. "Looks like you blew the drivetrain. That will
bring things to a halt quickly. Let me push this one out
of the way, and then I'll take you back in mine."*

*"That would be great," she said, starting toward her
cart. "I'm Delilah, by the way."*

*"Hey, there, Delilah," he said with a wink. "I bet
you've never heard that before."*

*"Oh, no," she agreed, helping him push the busted
cart off to the side. "Only once or ten thousand."*

*His laughter filled the air, and he brushed off his
hands. "Fair, but I've always loved the name. Just never
knew anyone with it before."*

"Well, now you do," she said, climbing into the passenger side of his cart. "Would you drop me off at the cafeteria? I was going to grab lunch, but I guess the cart decided I needed more exercise. Too many hours sitting at the computer."

"The cafeteria it is," he agreed. "I was headed there myself." He wasn't, but it was lunchtime, and he would take any chance to share lunch with a beautiful woman. His mama didn't raise no fool. Besides, Delilah intrigued him, and he knew nothing about her other than her name. *"I haven't seen you around the base before."*

"Just got here a few days ago," she answered with a shrug. "Pulled me in from a unit in Duluth stationed in Germany due to my skill set."

"No kidding?" he asked, nearly swerving off the road. "Duluth, Minnesota?"

"You betcha," she said with a cheesy grin.

"Small world. I'm out of Superior, Wisconsin."

"The good old Twin Ports. Looks like we have something in common, Lucas..."

"Ammunition Warrant Officer Lucas Porter," he said to finish the sentence. "What's your skill set? Must be big if they pulled you in for it."

"Looks like we have quite a bit in common. I'm a cyber warfare officer," she answered, with a flick of her eyes toward him. "Intel on ops. Maybe I shouldn't be telling you this stuff."

"You're fine. I work in munitions. My team plans those operations, and we provide the ammunition support. Looks like we go together like peanut butter and jelly."

Her laughter filled the cart, and Lucas couldn't help but chuckle, too. The way she tossed her head to the side,

allowing the sunshine to kiss her cheeks with freckles,
was too adorable not to notice. There was nothing about
Delilah he didn't like, but he knew better than to start
an on-base relationship. That was an excellent way to
get your heart broken—

"Luca?"

The name hit him and he snapped back to the present,
realizing the room had gone silent. He turned toward the
table where everyone sat expectantly. "Sorry, I got lost
in thought for a moment there. What was the question?"

"In a nutshell?" Cal asked, and Lucas nodded. "How
do you want to proceed?"

"Alone," he answered, and with one last look at Delilah, he walked out the door.

"I'LL GO TALK to him," Cal said as he stood.

Delilah held up her hand. "Give him a few minutes
to settle down. I knew he wouldn't react well to this,
but unfortunately, contacting him was my only choice."

"What's the big deal about his army duffel bag?"
Charlotte, Secure One's public liaison and Mack's girlfriend, asked. "Everyone around this table has one."

"True, but for Luca, it holds the reminders of what
happened that day on the base," Delilah explained. "All
of his medals went into it, too, because those remind him
of what he didn't do instead of what he did do."

"Medals?" Cal asked in surprise. "We had no idea
he had medals."

"That doesn't surprise me," Delilah said. "He doesn't
tell anyone. He refused to do anything more than have
them mailed to him. He never even opened the boxes,
just stuffed each one in the bag and walked away. I can't

remember them all, but one is the Purple Heart and the last one he got while I was with him was the Distinguished Service Cross."

Efren whistled low before he spoke. "That's not something you hear every day. I had no idea he was so decorated."

"Well—" she motioned at the door "—Luca likes it that way. That duffel bag is a time capsule that'll never be opened if he has anything to say about it. I tried to bring it with us to the VA hospital so that they could go through it with him, but he refused, adamantly so. Selfishly, I'm glad he's moved it with him over the years rather than dump it. I could never return to that part of the state to get the flash drive. I banked on the hope that, while he hated everything the bag represented, he would never get rid of it."

"I don't care what he says," Mina interrupted. "He's not doing this alone."

"She's right," Roman said. "The smart move would be for a team of us to retrieve the bag."

Delilah laughed loudly, and they all turned to stare at her. "Sorry," she said, momentarily putting her hand over her mouth. "But trust me. That will never happen. You saw his reaction to the idea that I even touched the bag to put the flash drive in the pocket. There's no way he'll let anyone else pick it up."

"You're saying Lucas is possessive of something he wants nothing to do with?" Marlise, who was Secure One's Client Coordinator and Cal's wife, often broke things down in a way that made it easy for everyone to understand.

"Everyone carries their ghosts differently, I guess.

Mine are wrapped up in the medal I sent him, and it's the only thing I carry from that time. If you knew the things he did that day, it would be easy to understand why he is the way he is. Right now, none of that matters. Top priority is convincing him to go with me to get that flash drive. I need to get out of here before all of you pay the price."

"I couldn't agree more," Cal said with a nod. "We'll prepare a plan to help you get to the storage unit and then find somewhere safe for you to go while we figure out who is after you. That somewhere will not be here."

"Understood," Delilah said with a nod. "Believe me when I say I never intended for any of this to happen or to drag all of you into this. I only wanted to get the drive and disappear again."

Mina's laughter filled the room as she shook her head. "You honestly thought you could contact Lucas the way you did and expect him to be like, 'Here's your flash drive. Bye,' as though the last six years hadn't happened?"

"You must understand that I was desperate," she said imploringly. "I didn't mean for any of this to happen or to drag Lucas back through his past. That's the last thing I wanted to do, but I was out of options."

Mina stood and walked around the table. "You have to stop apologizing, Delilah," she said, taking her elbow. "You're here now, which means you're one of us."

"We're called Secure One for a reason," Cal said from where he sat. "We are one under this roof, which means we are one for all and all for one. Right now, we are all for you, so this is what will happen. You'll help Lucas find the headspace he needs to be in while we make a plan. When he's ready, we'll be ready."

Mina walked Delilah to the door and leaned into her ear. "The only way out of this is through it, so start at the most important place. The beginning."

As Delilah walked out the conference room door, she couldn't help but think that was why they were in this spot to begin with.

Chapter Eight

Lucas sat in the dark kitchen with his head in his hands. His rhythmic breathing was second nature as Haven kept his paws on his leg and his muzzle under his handler's chin. If putting eyes on Lilah again wasn't enough of a shock, what she told him in that room pushed him past his breaking point.

"Luca," she said from the doorway, but he didn't look up. "I'm sorry. This was never supposed to happen. When I put the flash drive in the bag, it was for a week, not six years."

"It's the fact that you put it in there at all, Delilah. You knew how I felt about that bag."

"You need to get a grip, Luca," she said, and he snapped his head around to make eye contact. "Seriously. In the years since the war you've made yourself a new life here and found a brotherhood again. Yet, you continue to act like that bag is going to stand up and gun you down. I see all the work you've done to overcome everything that happened that day, and I respect the hell out of that, but you're not done. You can't have your life back until you open that bag and face the items inside."

"That's never going to happen."

"What are you so afraid of?" she asked, frustration loud and clear in her tone. "The memories? The idea that you saved lives and were commended for that?"

"I also took lives, Lilah. A whole lot of them."

"True, but they were trying to take yours and a whole lot of other Americans' lives."

"So that makes it right?"

"Luca, we both know there is nothing about war that is right to anyone with a decent moral compass. That doesn't mean we're given a choice. If you hadn't stepped up to be the hero that day—"

"Don't," he hissed from between his teeth. "Don't use that word."

"This is what I'm talking about," she said with a shake of her head. "Maybe you don't feel like one, but to me, you are. To the people you saved on that base that day, you are one. That doesn't mean you're flying through the sky with a cape. It means you stepped up when no one else would or could. That's what makes someone commendable. I understand that you're still mad all these years after you were put in that position, but it must be an awfully heavy load to carry every day."

"You don't know anything about it, Lilah."

"But I do. You always seem to forget I was also there. I live with the nightmares and the terror, too. My trauma may be different than yours, but that doesn't mean it's not there. None of this has been easy for me, either. The last thing I wanted was to be on the run for my life for six years, but here we are, aren't we? If I could go back and do things differently, I would, but I can't, so can we make a plan to get the drive? Without it, I'm a dead woman walking."

"Who are these people after you?" he asked, finally turning to face her again. If she wanted to read him the riot act about his choices in life, he could do the same. "You can't expect me to believe you have no idea who they are if this has gone on for six years."

"I honestly don't, Lucas. All I know is it has something to do with the antiquity cataloging."

"You swore you were only keeping the flash drive until Burris's trial."

"That was my plan, but again, I never returned to Superior for the flash drive. I was already on the run when the investigation ended without charges. I know you don't want to face that bag again, but it's time, don't you think?"

"You're not giving me a choice, are you, Lilah? You're just waltzing in with the demand that I do."

"There are no demands here, Luca," she said with a shake of her head. "Cal and Roman offered to go get the drive and leave the bag untouched. You're the one who said you were going alone."

"I don't want anyone around that bag but me."

"Do you keep that bag in the storage unit because you're afraid to face it or because you're afraid to live?"

He gazed at her in confusion for a moment. "What does that mean?"

"Every day that you keep that bag 'alive,'" she said, using air quotes, "is another day you can keep living in the past. From what I've seen about this place and its people, you could have a successful and fulfilling future if the past wasn't hanging around your neck like a dead albatross."

Lucas whistled while he shook his head. "Boy, you think you know a lot, don't you?"

"That's not what I think at all. The thing is, I know you, Luca. You can pretend that I don't or that the years we've been apart mean I can't possibly understand who you are now, but that's all it is—pretending. I know who you are to your core," she whispered, tapping her finger on his chest.

Lucas grabbed her finger and held it tightly. He tried to tell himself it was because she was annoying him, but the truth was, he wanted to touch her. He wanted to feel her warmth again after all these years. He wanted her to see how much he'd changed and the improvements he'd made in his life.

She can't do that if you don't show her those things. You're behaving the same way you did six years ago. Be the man she needs right now.

The thought halted his count of three, and he pulled in one breath and held it. The voice was right. He wasn't showing Delilah that he'd changed since she left. If anything, he was proving to her that he hadn't moved anywhere or learned anything about himself since they were last together. The very idea stiffened his spine. He stood, holding his hand out.

"Can I trust you, Delilah Hartman?" What he didn't ask was if he could trust her not to break his heart.

"You can, Luca. I know how much I hurt you by disappearing from your life, but know that was the last thing I wanted to happen. The choice was run and protect you, or stay and risk them trying to get to me through you. I couldn't let that happen."

"Then let's do what we've always done best."

Lilah lifted a brow, and it brought a smile to his lips.

"The one thing we did best probably shouldn't be done right now, Luca."

This time, he couldn't help but laugh when he chucked her gently under the chin. "Let me rephrase that. The second thing we did best."

"Work together?"

"That," he agreed, taking her hand. "We were always a great team. Maybe that was practice for what was to come."

"For the time when it would be imperative to know each other's strengths and weaknesses?"

"And that time is now," he finished. "Let's find out what the team has planned, get that flash drive and win your life back."

Delilah leaned into him, resting her head on his shoulder. "Thank you, Luca. I hate that I've stirred all of this up for you again."

"No," he whispered, holding her gaze for a beat. "Thank you for reminding me that I'm standing in front of the person who changed my life six years ago and the person I wanted to change my life for back then. I have changed, and now it's time to prove it."

"And I'm standing in front of the person who changed my life six years ago and the person I was protecting all this time. I don't regret losing out on those years because you were safe, but I'm glad we have this time together, even if it's fraught with danger."

"Me, too, even if it looks different than the life we planned." He led her toward the door. "Haven, forward," he called to the dog. Once they got to the doorway, he paused. "I will still do everything in my power to protect you, Lilah. That means whatever needs to be done, I'll do."

"There's the Luca I knew was in there," she said, dropping one lid down in a wink.

THE DARKNESS SWALLOWED them as they slid from the van parked southwest of the storage units. They hadn't picked up a tail as far as they could tell, and Lucas had been in constant contact with the other two cars that held Secure One teams running diversions. She and Lucas planned to slide in, get the flash drive, head back to the van and drive to a small motel an hour away from the Canadian border. Once they had the flash drive, they couldn't go back to headquarters, but Mina sent a laptop and equipment for Delilah to communicate with her once the flash drive was in their possession.

Delilah glanced over at Lucas, who was gauging the distance they had to walk without cover. Trees surrounded the storage facility on three sides, leaving the only unprotected side at the driveway approach.

"My unit is in the back corner. If we stay in the trees until we're opposite it, the only time we'll be exposed is the time it takes to unlock the door."

"All of this cloak and dagger stuff might be a bit much, Luca," she whispered as they walked, Haven glued to his handler's side, step for step. This time, the dog was wearing his bulletproof vest, too. "Lately, it has taken them four or five days to find me."

"Maybe, but that was before the island. Now they know who you're with, so I'm not taking any chances."

"Fair enough," Delilah said, but she still thought it was unnecessary. It would take that team on the island a long time to regroup and relocate her. They hadn't been at Secure One longer than three hours before the team had a plan and implemented it.

Another hundred yards farther, and Lucas pulled her to a stop. "The unit is right there," he said, pointing at the metal building in front of them. Not surprisingly, strings of Christmas lights hung from the eaves of the metal buildings. It offered a little light in the darkness, and it slowed her pounding heart. "As soon as I open the side walk-through door, you get inside. I'm not going to mess with the roll-up door. That leaves us too visible."

"Why don't I just wait here?" she asked, leaning into his ear to speak now that he had her spooked. "The flash drive is in the outside pocket—"

"I can't prevent a sneak attack if you're in the woods and I'm not. We're a team and we stay together."

"Ten-four," she whispered with a smile he couldn't see. They were a team. It hadn't taken much to remind him of that.

Lucas gestured to Haven and slid out of the woods like a ghost. It was easy to see his time at Secure One had taught him new skills that she suspected took a lot of practice. Especially since he took Haven with him everywhere. He had the door open by the time she reached him, and he practically shoved her through the small opening, followed her in with Haven and closed the door with barely a click.

Lucas flicked a flashlight on and shone it around the space. One glance was all she needed to see that the only thing in the storage unit was the bag. Rather than comment on it, she glanced up at him.

"The side pocket," she said as Lucas knelt over the

bag. She noticed him hesitate with his hand over the pocket. She crouched and put her hand on his shoulder. "You got this," she whispered. "Baby steps."

He nodded as he breathed in and waited, then blew it out and reached for the pocket just as the first bullet slammed into the metal unit.

"Dammit!" Lucas hissed, grabbing her and shoving her behind him as another bullet hit the side door. It was a steel door but wouldn't hold bullets back for long. They were trapped in a tin box and had no way out except through the steel curtain roll-up door, which was padlocked from the outside.

"Stay down," Lucas yelled, and she could tell he was running their options through his head. They didn't have many other than praying the steel door held. "Get down on your belly and get to the back of the unit. It's protected by the opposite one! When they hit that rolling door, it will give quickly. I'll get one chance to end them before they end us."

Delilah was pulling Haven down by her when the shooting stopped. "Now," Lucas hissed, moving with her to the back of the unit until a sound stopped them in their tracks.

"Secure one, Charlie," Cal called through the door.

"Secure two, Lima!" Lucas answered, scrambling to the side door and throwing it open. "Cal! Are you alone?"

"Not a chance," Roman said, stepping out of the woods.

"I thought we were screwed six ways to Sunday until you called out. You guys being here wasn't part of the plan."

"It always was, son," Cal said while they checked the

pulses on the four guys on the ground. "We didn't want you to argue about us coming along for the ride. If you didn't need us, you never had to know we were here."

"I probably would have argued, but I'm sure glad you're here."

"Four this time," Delilah said, stepping around Lucas. "They're upping the ante."

"All carrying ARs," Cal said as he got to the final guy. "Got a live one." He grabbed a pair of restraints and cuffed him.

"These three have gone on to the great hellscape beyond," Roman answered. "No IDs. No anything other than their weapons."

"Did you find the drive?" Cal asked, standing up to address Lucas.

"I was just reaching for the bag when they started shooting. They had to be hot on our heels by no more than minutes. How did they find us so quickly?" Lucas turned to her. "What did you bring from your last place?"

"Nothing," she swore, holding up her hands. "I bought everything new before I went to the island, including undergarments."

"I don't understand it," Lucas said. "They're tracking you somehow. Your glasses?"

She shook her head. "I buy new ones every time I move, and always from a different online provider."

"What are we going to do with these guys?" Roman asked, interrupting Lucas's train of thought.

"Well, we can't exactly hide this," Cal motioned around the area with his hands. "Shall we claim it was a shoot-out at Christmas corral?" Lucas grunted with laughter, something he didn't think he was capable of at the moment. His laughter brought a smile to Cal's lips, too. "I'll call the cops, and we'll say we were working security when we heard the ruckus."

"How are you going to explain the bullet holes in them?" Roman asked with a smirk.

"We've got a live one here. Since he's unconscious, we blame it on him. He can sort it out when he's awake, alert and oriented."

"I just want to know who they are and what they want with me!" Delilah exclaimed, frustration evident in her voice.

Lucas ran to her and put his arm around her shoulder while Haven moved in and propped his snout under her elbow. "It's okay. We'll figure this out," he promised, helping her over to where Cal and Roman stood. "Same plan?"

Cal nodded. "Take the van to the motel while we handle this situation. Once you're there safely, call in. Mack and Efren report that these were the only guys in the area, so your walk to the van is clear. Lucas, grab your bag."

"We only need the flash drive," he said, headed toward the doorway, but Cal grabbed his arm.

"The cops will be crawling around here in about an hour. Take the whole bag, or it will become evidence. What else is in the unit that's tied to your name?"

Delilah noticed Lucas's spine stiffen as he considered Cal's words. "Nothing. The only thing in it is the bag. I rented the unit online under a different name and a PO Box."

Cal nodded once as he glanced around the units. "It looks like Sal invested in Christmas lights instead of security cameras, so that helps. Get the bag and get out. We'll take care of everything else."

The door was open, so Delilah watched Lucas stare at the bag for a full thirty seconds before he slowly bent over and picked it up. When he stood, the expression on his face was unlike any she'd seen before. It was determination mixed with something else. Pride? Hatred? Pain? Maybe all of the above. As he strode toward her, the look intensified until he took her hand.

"We'll be in touch once we're safe. Give us three hours. I want to be sure we don't pick up a tail."

"I've got GPS on the van, so we'll keep a close eye on it. I would send a follow team, but I don't want to make your identity obvious."

"I've got this," Lucas assured his boss. "Hopefully, we can get a few hours head start before the next team is sent out."

"There will be a next team," Delilah added, glancing at Cal and Roman. "Watch yourselves."

"Haven, forward," Lucas ordered, and the dog lined up beside his leg. "Lima, out," he said as they entered the tree line.

Delilah jogged through the woods next to Lucas, but they never spoke. As he held the bag tightly, it was like watching him be reborn. The bag used to be the enemy, but now, he was ready to make peace with it.

Then he glanced at her, and the look in his eyes said that was the furthest thing from the truth.

Chapter Nine

"The dome light is disabled. Climb in while I get Haven situated," Lucas whispered to Delilah once he cleared the van of interlopers. While she settled in the front, Lucas slid open the side door and lowered the sizeable duffel bag to the floor. He struggled to unclench his fist of its prize. It wasn't that the bag was physically heavy, but emotionally, it weighed more than he could carry. This time, he hadn't been given a choice. He had to carry the weight for her. If what she said was true, she'd been fighting this war alone for the last six years. She needed a team to back her up now.

He hooked Haven into his seat, slammed the door and jumped in the driver's side. "Buckle up."

Delilah slid her seat belt over her chest while he started the van. "Did you find the flash drive?"

"Didn't look," he answered, straightening his seat belt. "It's hidden in the bag right now. We'll leave it until we get to the motel. If we get into an altercation on the road, I'd rather it wasn't on your person."

"They won't find us that fast," she said, turning in her seat to look at the bag.

"That's what you said about the guys we just took

out." Lucas was ready to put the van in Drive when something Cal said sent a zap of fear through his gut. "GPS."

Delilah's look was curious. "What about it? Cal said he was tracking the van. That can only help us if we encounter more resistance."

"What did you bring from Secure One?" he asked, leaving the van in Park and turning to her.

After glancing down at herself, she met his gaze. "Just the clothes Mina gave me and the issued equipment Cal insisted I take, like the handgun and cuffs. Mina gave me a new lip gloss and a few toiletries. The only other thing I have is my identification, which is fake, and my medal."

Disgust slithered through Lucas's belly at the thought running through his mind. "Do you keep the medal with you all the time, or do you normally leave it in a safety deposit box?"

She shook her head immediately. "It's always with me, since I'm never in the same place very long."

Lucas swallowed back the bile in his throat and held out his hand. "Can I see it?"

"Why?" she asked, digging inside her jacket pocket for a moment before she pulled it out. "It hasn't changed since you gave it back to me."

Once it was in his hand, he ran his fingers over the medal, looking for bumps or outcroppings. "That's what has been bugging me, Lilah," he explained, holding up the medal. "You carried this everywhere and they kept finding you. You sent it to me, and I showed up on the island with extra visitors. You have it in your pocket tonight and they're on us in minutes. They're using the medal to track you."

"Impossible," she whispered with a shake of her head.

"There's no way there's a tracker small enough to put in that medal. Not to mention, I've had it for six years. The battery would never last."

"Nothing is impossible if it's the military tracking you. You'd be surprised by the tech they have that no one knows about, including solar-powered trackers."

"You can't prove it, though." She motioned at the medal in his hand. "And we don't have time to take it apart."

"Don't need to, as long as it doesn't go with us."

He climbed out of the van and dug a hole with his multi-tool deep enough to lay the medal in and cover it up. He took a picture with the Secure One phone and sent it to Cal with a message before he climbed back into the van. She stared at him with her lips pulled in a thin line.

"I'm sorry, Lilah, but we can't take it with us. Just in case. I sent the information to Cal to get the medal and move it somewhere." He pulled the lever into Drive and left the curb, knowing there were still over two hours to go in this long night. "He'll keep watch on it. If another group of armed guys shows up at the location, it's a good bet the medal is to blame."

"That doesn't make sense, though, Luca," she said, leaning back in the seat with her arms crossed. "Why would the military want to track me? I've been discharged free and clear for years."

"Let me ask you. Who else knows about these antiquities being in the States?"

"Now? I don't know. Back then, only my boss, his boss and the museum curators."

"Which tells me it was a top-secret operation at the

time. That means you are one of the few people with the information in your head."

"I'm probably the only one with it in my head, but my boss and his bosses have access to that information, too," she said, throwing up her hands. "I had to transmit the information daily to the person in charge of the shipments."

"I could be dead wrong about everything," he said to appease her, but he was convinced the medal was to blame. "It's just a better-safe-than-sorry situation. If we don't have the medal with us, and the guys find us again, then we know it wasn't the medal."

"All I know is, I'm exhausted," she said, staring out the back window as though she expected headlights to pop up and mow them down. "I've been running for so many years, all over the country. It isn't conducive to having any quality of life." She turned around in the seat and slumped down into her coat.

Lucas reached over and turned up the heat. "I wish I hadn't been so angry with you and had tried harder to find you when I got out," he whispered, squeezing her shoulder. "When the information didn't come easily, I gave up. It was easier to convince myself that you didn't want me to find you, and it was better to let you go, than it was to fight against the memories of us."

"It wasn't easy staying off the internet," she admitted with a tip of her head. "It required burner phones, lots of fake identifications and some pretty shady living situations."

"But no matter what you did, they kept coming for you?"

"They always found me. Sometimes it was weeks or

months, and one time it was a year, but whoever they are, they're great at keeping me unbalanced and unhinged."

"You aren't unhinged," he corrected her as he steered the van down the two-lane highway. "You're scared and confused. After being attacked like that, it had to be difficult to trust anyone."

"I didn't trust anyone. In hindsight, I should have trusted you, Luca."

Lucas heard the slur to her words, and he turned the radio up as Frank Sinatra crooned about having a merry little Christmas. He glanced away from the road for a split second to see her sinking into sleep, comforted by the warmth of the van and the company of another person after so many years alone. They were both exhausted, so he'd let her sleep while they found their way to safety—at least for a little while—and then he'd sit her down and get the real story. The guys they'd come across screamed military to him, and that scared him more than anything else would. If the government wanted her, they'd have her. Lucas could do nothing to stop it.

LILAH WOKE WITH a start to realize the van had stopped moving. She glanced at the old blue building in front of her and then to her left, where Lucas sat in the driver's seat, grasping the steering wheel with an iron grip.

"We made it," she said, stretching in the seat. "I didn't mean to fall asleep. You should have woken me so I could keep watch."

"It wasn't a problem, Lilah," he said, his gaze firmly planted on the building beyond the windshield. "The drive was uneventful and I had some thinking to do, anyway. I need to go check in. The second I close the door, move to the driver's seat and keep the van running. If anyone approaches you, get out of here."

"I can't just leave you!" she exclaimed, turning in her seat.

"You can and you will. The van is being tracked in the control room, and we'll catch up with you."

"What about Haven?"

"He's coming with me, of course. If everything is safe, we'll return to the van once I clear the room. Ten-four?"

"Heard and acknowledged," she agreed, waiting for him to unhook Haven from his seat belt. After he checked all sides of the van, he climbed out, and Haven hopped over the console and out of the van to follow his handler.

The moment the locks engaged, fear drove Lilah to climb into the driver's seat and put her hands on the wheel. She had to stay on her toes and shut out the memories of the last time she was in a place like this with Luca. It had been a beautiful summer day, and they'd been driving up the north shore along Lake Superior. Their destination had been Thunder Bay, but they had no schedule to follow or place to be. They'd come across this little town, well, you couldn't call it a town as much as a place you passed through on the road to somewhere else. Luca had seen the blue brick building and steered the car into the parking lot—

The locks disengaged and Lilah jumped. Her attention captured by the memories, she totally missed Luca returning to the van. She was lucky no one else approached her while she was daydreaming. "All clear," he said, grabbing their bags from the back. He helped her out of the van before he propelled her into the small room. He closed the door, threw the lock, drew the curtains and dropped the bags on the floor. "I need to let the team know we made it."

"You said they were tracking the van. Aren't they already aware?"

Rather than answer her, he pushed past her and grabbed a gear bag, unzipping it and pulling out computer equipment. She left him for a moment to use the bathroom. The shower beckoned her, so she stripped from her dusty clothes and stepped under the warm spray. She forced the memories of a long-ago time in a place like this where she and Luca had shared the shower—had shared everything—and focused on the present. She couldn't help but wonder if what Luca thought about the medal was true. In hindsight, it was the only thing she always had with her when she moved from place to place. The sticking point for her was, if someone was tracking her with the medal, that could only mean one thing. They had to be military. She couldn't think of any reason why the military would track her or accost her. They didn't even know the flash drive existed.

But you exist.

The thought jarred her, and she dropped the soap bar on the floor. She stooped to pick it up and thought back to the day she'd found the secret file on the server. There was no identifying information as to who had put it there, but there was also no way anyone knew she had a copy. She'd covered her digital trail over there to avoid being picked up by the enemy, who were always looking for a way to start a cyberwar. There was no way anyone could know she'd seen that file, right?

A cold shudder went through her even as she stood under the hot water. None of this made sense. She was distracted and jumpy, which made her feel out of control and scattered. It didn't help that she was continually trapped in small spaces with the man she'd loved for years, all while knowing she could never have him. Not as long as she was being hunted. There was no way she would be the one to remind him of the things he tried to forget.

It's too late for that.

Slamming the water off, Lilah huffed at that voice. She was starting to hate it, mainly because it was always right. It was too late to protect Luca from the memories of that time. As she dried herself, part of her wondered if that was such a bad thing. He'd told her he learned how to work around the memories of what happened to him, not that he'd dealt with them head-on. She was well aware through personal experience that confronting them wasn't going to make them go away, but not being afraid of how each memory ended, because she already knew what was coming, did make it easier to let them roll over her and fall away rather than roll over her and drown her.

Lilah tucked the towel under her armpit and glanced at herself in the minuscule mirror over the sink. "That may not be the case for Luca, and you know that. The things he saw and did are incomprehensible to most people."

With a tip of her shoulder, she gathered her clothes off the floor. Maybe that was why he learned to work around them rather than face them. Talking about those things, admitting to what he did that day to ensure his fellow soldiers got off that base, might make everything worse.

When she opened the door, Lucas had finished with

the devices he'd laid out on the small desk against the bathroom wall. "Are there clean clothes in any of those bags, or should I put these back on?"

He spun as though he hadn't heard her come out but came to an abrupt halt when he saw her wrapped in only a towel. He cleared his throat before he spoke. "Enjoy your shower?"

"I did, but don't worry, I left you plenty of hot water."

"I'm not worried about the hot water. I am worried about you. You're hurt," he said, stepping forward and tracing a large bruise on her shoulder.

She glanced down at his finger on her skin. He left a trail of deep yearning that burned her skin with every inch. She deserved the pain of the bruise and to withstand his touch, knowing his hands would never be on her as a lover.

"It's fine. I must have hurt it on the island and didn't realize it. What did Secure One say?"

Luca shook his head as though the question snapped him back to reality. "The cops bought their story and took over the scene, but not before Cal snapped pictures of the guys' faces. Mina was able to use facial recognition to identify them. They're all ex-military."

Lilah's heart sank as she sucked in air. "Dammit. I've been telling myself there's no way they could be military. This doesn't make any sense, Luca."

"They aren't military. They're ex-military, but that raises the question of who they're working for now."

"Good point," Lilah agreed, sinking to the bed in the center of the room. "I'm no closer to figuring this out now than I was six years ago."

"You haven't had time to figure it out," he said, kneeling beside her. "You've been too busy trying to stay alive, right?"

"Which would have been easier if I knew who was after me and why," she admitted to the man who was much too close for her liking. All she had to do was turn her head, and she could have her lips on his. She resisted by staring straight ahead at the door.

"We'll get to the bottom of this so you can have your life back," Lucas promised. "Mina is working on things now and will keep us posted."

"What life?" she asked with a shake of her head. "I have no life, Luca. I haven't since the day I left you and ran headlong into the night. The cut on my chin turned the car into a crime scene, so I had hoped by abandoning it, they would think Delilah Hartman had died a tragic death. How wrong I'd been. Getting to the bottom of this means I'm free, but I'm thirty-four years old and have no idea how to live a normal life."

They sat in silence, their gazes locked together, and Lilah wondered if he was thinking about the last time they were together in a place like this. She couldn't force her mind away from those memories, even as they heated her cheeks and sent waves of sensation through her belly, then lower to the place she had shared with no one since she lost him. Back then, Luca had been a fast and furious lover. It was rare that they took their time, even if they tried. The heat built too quickly and drove them to touch, taste and tease each other as fast as they could until the explosive end.

"Do you remember the last time we were in this motel?" Luca's question pulled her out of her daydreams and back to reality.

"I haven't stopped thinking about it since I opened my eyes in the van. It feels like we were in a motel like this just yesterday with fewer, or maybe different, worries."

"Not a different motel. If it were daylight, you'd realize this is the same motel, on the same road, just not the same room."

"You mean, this is—"

"Yes," he answered, dropping his knee to the floor. "Mina picked it. I had no idea it was the same place until I realized it could be the only place."

Lilah's fingers traced his five o'clock shadow, and the rasp against her skin reminded her how he felt against her as they made love. "If you're uncomfortable, we can keep driving."

"I'm not uncomfortable," he promised, his hand capturing hers against his cheek. "At least not in the memory department. In the 'being trapped in a motel with an almost naked woman who I know can blow my mind the moment I put my lips on hers' department, I'm uncomfortable."

Instinctively, she tightened her grip around the towel. "I'm sorry. Let me get dressed so we can focus."

"You think we'll be able to focus just because you put clothes on, or do you think no matter what we do, being here together is a walk down memory lane we need to take?"

"Are you saying what I think you're saying?"

He tipped his head in agreement. "Once and done. Get it out of our system so we can focus on the case without this constant pull between us."

He was dead wrong if he thought falling into bed with him once would stop that pull between them. Lilah wasn't sure years of falling into bed with him would stop that pull, but she had to ask herself if she wanted to be with him one more time or if she wanted to remember who they were together before all of this happened.

Her decision made, she stood and walked into the bathroom, the memory of the days those brown eyes were hers too much to bear.

Chapter Ten

Lucas watched Lilah close the bathroom door to shut him out. He knew it was a risk to suggest they make love again, but he was scared. He was scared that the connection between them was stronger than ever and the only way for him to know for sure was to be with her in the most elemental way. If the connection was just as strong as it was six years ago, he had to rethink how he'd been living. Delilah's reappearance was going to put a crimp in his ability to live in the land of denial he'd so firmly planted himself in at that hospital when she never showed again.

He stood and glanced at Haven, who lay on a makeshift bed of blankets in the corner. The dog kept his eyes on him but didn't approach, which meant he didn't think his handler needed him. Yet. That time could come, but for now, Lucas raised his hand and knocked on the bathroom door. "Lilah? Come out and talk to me. You don't even have any clothes in there."

Her heavy sigh from the other side of the door made him smile. She always hated it when he used logic to thwart her emotions. She told him it took her out of the moment and forced her to think instead of feel. That's what he needed her to do right now. Think. Research. React. Participate. She couldn't do that if there was a constant wall between them.

The doorknob turned, and the door swung open. She held his gaze as she walked out and motioned at the bags. "Which one is mine? I'll get dressed."

"Sit," he said instead, motioning at the bed. "If we don't clear the air between us, working together as a team will be impossible." What he didn't say was working with her was tasking his emotions, and clearing the air wouldn't help that, but it would, hopefully, help her. Once she was sitting, he pulled the blanket up and wrapped it around her shoulders, then he sat next to her. "You're walking on eggshells around me. That can't continue."

"I'm trying not to upset you," she whispered, her eyes on the floor until he tipped her chin to face him.

"Stop doing that," he ordered, and her gaze snapped to his. "I'm not emotionally labile the way I was the last time we were together. I don't snap the way I used to. I've learned how to manage my emotions in a way that doesn't hurt anyone, including myself."

"I'm glad," she said with a smile. "I could tell how different you were the moment you showed up on the island. That's not why I'm being cautious."

"I don't understand then, Lilah. Explain it to me."

He watched her tighten the blanket around her chest and drop her gaze again. He let her, for now, in case it was the only way she could talk about what she was going through. "I need help, and I can't—"

"Make me angry, or I might stop helping you?" He'd interrupted her in hopes of taking her by surprise. She could say whatever she wanted and he wouldn't know if he could believe it. If he told the truth, there would be no way she could hide her reaction from him. The fact that she hadn't looked up and continued to stare at the floor told him he was right. He tipped her chin up again and cocked a smile across his lips. "You're stuck with me, kid."

"I don't want you to feel obligated, Luca," she said in a whisper. "I can take the flash drive and go. Then I'm no longer your problem."

"Not exactly true," he said, that smile faltering. "We're connected now. Whoever is after you knows that. Besides, you've been my problem for many years, so now that you're back, I can't let you walk out the door while you're in danger."

"I've been your problem?"

His stomach roiled at the question. If he answered it honestly, he would hurt her. If he lied, he hurt himself. Gazing into her eyes, he decided this one time, he could take the pain. "As I told you, I looked for you over the years, Lilah. I went from a man in love, to a man who was hurt, to a man who was worried, to a man who was numb."

"I wanted to contact you, Luca, so badly—"

"But you couldn't, or you'd put me at risk, too."

"Truthfully, I couldn't be sure of that, but I had to assume that if you were connected to me in any way, you'd be in danger. I didn't want you to live the way I had to live. Going from town to town, seedy apartment to seedy apartment. Low-wage job to day work here and there. Spending time in the forests surviving on fish and rabbits as I moved across the countryside."

"That doesn't sound like any kind of life."

"It wasn't, but I had to keep moving or risk being captured again. If you're right about the medal, they must laugh at my stupidity whenever they come after me."

"No," he said, taking her hand between his. "You knew you were being tracked, but you didn't know how, so there was no reason for you to suspect it was the medal."

"I was so careful with everything else, Luca. If I hadn't let my pride overrule my common sense, I would have put the medal in a safety deposit box and walked away. The thought never crossed my mind."

"Was it pride that made you hold on to that medal?" She didn't answer, so he pushed her a bit. "Was it, Lilah? Or was it something else?"

"That ceremony was the last time you told me you were proud of me before I dropped you at that hospital and abandoned you!" she exclaimed, tears shimmering in her eyes. "I abandoned you. For that, you should never forgive me, Lucas Porter."

"Wrong," he insisted, wiping away a stray tear that fell lazily down her cheek. "You didn't abandon me. You left me somewhere safe with every intention of returning, right?" Her nod was enough for him. "You couldn't control what happened after that to either one of us, so you have to stop carrying guilt about it. Was I upset and angry in the beginning? Yes. Have I been angry at you all of these years? No. I locked away every emotion I didn't need to live in the outside world into a box. That box was locked tight until I got called to a funeral home to collect the ashes of the woman I thought I'd love forever. That's when the box broke open again."

"I wish so many things, Luca," she whispered. "The biggest thing I wish is that I could have spared you all of that pain. That I could have gotten you a message somehow or someway, but I couldn't risk it."

"Because you didn't want me to get hurt, right?" he asked, thumbing away another tear. Her tears always broke his heart, and tonight was no different because, once again, she was crying over him.

"Yes, of course. I couldn't risk that my message would lead them to you and they'd hurt you to get to me. Can you ever forgive me, Luca? I mean, truly forgive me for all of this."

"There's nothing to forgive, Lilah. That's what you aren't grasping. You didn't start this. But what you did after it began, you did out of love. I know that, sometimes, doing something out of love is the hardest thing of all." Like pretending for the rest of his life that he no longer needed this woman to feel alive. "Carrying around anger about it only wastes energy we could be using to find the guys after you and end it so you can live again. Right here, right now, you have to let the guilt go. You've carried it too long and for no reason. The biggest thing they taught me at the VA was to let go of anything that didn't serve to improve your life. This guilt and shame you're carrying doesn't improve your life. It keeps you from staying present and being my partner as we try to navigate who's after you and why. Do you understand what I'm trying to say?"

Lilah never answered him with words. She purposefully leaned forward until their lips connected. A bright light exploded behind his eyes, and he dragged her to him. The sensation of her lips on his had been a memory for so long. Her body, soft and warm under his hands, moved against him in familiar ways as his tongue probed her lips to take the kiss back to days gone by. The moment he slipped his tongue between those sweet lips, he knew she hadn't put their past behind her, either.

"Lilah." The word fell from his lips as he kissed his way down her neck toward the towel that had slipped, teasing him with the imagery of her sweet body. "You're so beautiful."

She jerked, grasped the towel and tried to push him away all in one movement. It was more knee-jerk than intentional, so he held her still. "We can't do this," she finally gasped.

"Feels to me like we should," he answered, holding her gaze so she knew he was fully engaged with her. "We're explosive together, Lilah, and we don't want that explosion to happen at the wrong time and put us at risk. We're safe here tonight. After that, I can't promise anything."

She pushed herself off his lap and grabbed a bag off the floor. "That's where you're wrong. We aren't safe here. Those guys could surround this place as we sit here letting our hormones run away with our common sense. You're a security guy. You know I'm right. That," she said, motioning at the bed she'd just leaped from, "will never happen again." The slamming of the bathroom door punctuated her sentence, leaving him to do nothing but stare after her and wonder where he had gone wrong.

THE KEYBOARD CLACKED as Lilah finished sending her message to Mina. She wanted to know if they could track the men at the storage unit to any particular employer or if they were more of a thugs-for-hire situation. Knowing they were ex-military explained their ability to penetrate her defenses without fail, but that didn't explain who they worked for or what they wanted. She had to know who was giving the orders if she was ever going to solve this problem and move on with her life.

A quick flick of her gaze to Luca told her that may never be possible. At least not fully moving on. Having her lips on his was as explosive as it ever was until she remembered she wasn't the same woman he had made love to in this motel the last time. She wanted him to remember her body the way it was then rather than see her body now. There was nothing beautiful about her anymore—body, mind or spirit.

Unfortunately, she had hurt him by reacting the way she did without explanation. That couldn't be helped. What he didn't know was helping him move on with his life. She could only make him understand that with deeds and not words. Luca had a future, a promising future where he could help others. She didn't. She lived in the moment, knowing any moment could be her last.

He'd been standing by the window for the last hour, peering through a crack in the curtain. He had his gun out and at his side with his spine ramrod straight, or as straight as it would go since he broke it trying to defend the base all those years ago. He never talked about how he had broken multiple vertebrae in his back that day or how lucky he was that it never impinged the spinal cord. They were able to stabilize his spine, and with six months of physical therapy, he could now do most things again. It appeared he had a new health regimen that kept him in far better shape than when she left him at the VA, too.

She didn't need him to tell her that lifting weights was part of his workout routine. She liked that he cared for himself and knew he mattered to others who depended on him. That hadn't been the case for the longest time.

She pushed herself up from the desk chair and walked closer to him, still keeping a healthy distance so she didn't throw herself at him again. "We should get the flash drive while we wait."

Luca turned from the window and stuck his gun into the holster at his back. "I'll grab it for you." His steps were stilted, but he reached the bag and stuck his hand into the pocket, feeling around. "It's not here."

"What?" Her heart started racing, and she ran to him, grabbed the strap and tossed it on the bed. She didn't care if he liked it or not. If her bargaining chip was gone, she was as good as dead. She didn't know much, but she did know that. Whoever this was, they weren't hunting her for funsies. She stuck her hand into the pocket and felt around, her pent-up breath releasing when her finger entered the bag's main compartment. "There's a hole," she said, looking up at Lucas, watching her closely with his hands in fists. "It had to have fallen into the main compartment."

"There shouldn't be a hole in it. It's been untouched for years."

"Luca, you've had it in an unprotected storage unit surrounded by woods. Chances are a mouse found its way in. You should probably brace yourself for what's inside, both from the memories and the fact that some of it may now be in a mouse's nest."

She stepped away and let him be the one to unhook the strap and open the bag. It opened at the top, so he had to remove each item to get to the bottom. Soon, the bed was covered in his fatigues, dress uniform, medals and boots. He pulled a wooden box out that fell open when he set it on the bed. Inside were letters, the envelopes dirty and wrinkled.

"Letters?" she asked, glancing up at him. She knew better than to reach for them. There was little Lucas was territorial of other than the contents of this bag.

"From my mom," he agreed, running a finger across the top of one. "She died when I was at the training facility with Haven."

"Did you go to her funeral?"

"The hospice center called and told me it was time to come say my final goodbyes. The school packed up Haven and sent a trainer with me for the two-hour trip to Rochester. I was with her when she took her final breath. She asked me to wear my dress uniform to her funeral, but that was a final wish I couldn't grant."

She grasped his elbow, hoping it would keep him grounded in the room with her. "I'm sure it mattered more to her that you were there with her at the end, Luca. I'm proud of you for going to her when she needed you."

"Our relationship had always been strained," he agreed, staring at the letters. "I was always surprised when a letter would arrive from her. She could have sent an email, but she went to the trouble of writing a letter and mailing it every time."

"A mother's love is like that," Lilah said, gently rubbing his shoulder. "She wanted you to know she cared."

"Some might say a day late and a dollar short, but I tried not to look at it like that," he said, closing the box with a click. "She did her best with what she had, and that wasn't much of anything. Mom was who she was, but by the time I went into the service, she was clean again and had found stable work and an apartment."

"Then the dementia struck."

"And it struck hard," he agreed with a nod. "Mom was barely fifty-five when she died, but I always knew the years of drug abuse would come back to haunt her."

"I'm glad you got to make amends with her, or at the very least, you were together when she took her last breath as you were when you took your first."

His lips turned up in a smile, and he glanced at her for the first time since she'd pushed him away. "Now, that is truly a Delilah Hartman statement. You always had a way of summing everything up in the neatest bow."

"I don't know if that's a compliment or a knock."

"A compliment. I always appreciated your ability to eliminate all the noise so I could hear the truth." Rather than continue speaking, he eyed her as though he were challenging her to do the same now, but she couldn't. Wouldn't. Not when their lives were on the line. Once she knew he was safe, she could leave him to live the life he'd built without her. A life he had worked hard for and didn't need her screwing up more than she already had.

"I don't see any evidence of a mouse yet. Or my flash drive," she said, returning them to the business at hand.

"There's not much left in here." He pulled out his army-issued winter coat, and a black rectangle fell to the floor.

Delilah scooped it up and held it to her chest with an exhale. "We got it." She held her hand out, revealing a high-tech drive. "Now we just have to hope the information on it isn't corrupt."

"What are the numbers for?" he asked, pointing at the buttons on the outside of the flash drive.

"A passcode to open it. This drive encrypts the information as you transfer it to keep the information secure."

"Do you remember the passcode?" Lucas asked as she walked past him toward the computer.

"Of course. I used a number I could never forget." She typed in a sequence and pulled the cover off the top of it. "Your birthday."

Chapter Eleven

Lucas's gaze roved over the bed that now held his old life. The uniforms. The boots. The medals. All the things he wanted to forget but couldn't. They stared back at him in judgment. They weren't judging him, though. Only a human could pass judgment, and he was excellent at being his own judge and jury. He couldn't help but wonder if his judgment of himself had been too harsh. Truthfully, he'd played judge, jury and executioner for so long he wasn't sure how to stop.

You can't have your life back until you open that bag and face the items inside. What are you so afraid of?

The words she'd said floated through his mind. He'd done what he had always believed was the impossible. He'd opened the bag and was again face-to-face with his past. That meant only the last question remained. What was he afraid of and why? When and why did he give this bag the power over him? He wasn't even wearing these clothes or boots when the base fell. Those items were cut off him and destroyed at the hospital in Germany.

The bag was on the floor, and he picked it up, sticking his hand into the pocket to pull out his discharge papers. He read them, his unconscious mind forcing him into the triangle breathing as he did so. He read every word, letting them pulse boldly in his head before shrinking back to normal. Each word released a little bit of hold the bag had on him. Each paragraph he finished snapped a bind that had tied him to it for years. When he finished, he slid them back into the envelope, ready to put them back in the bag. Something stopped him. Instead, he slipped them into the side pocket of his cargo pants and lifted the medals from the bed.

They had arrived in the mail each time he refused to go to the ceremony, and went directly into the bag. He never even opened the boxes to look at the medals. What was the point? Pieces of metal and ribbon didn't change what he did to earn them. Earn them. How ridiculous did that sound? It was a way to pretty up the fact that he had killed for them. Bled for them. Hurt for them. He didn't want to be remembered for any of that.

It means you stepped up when no one else would or could. That's what makes someone commendable.

All of the therapy he'd gone through hadn't had the same effect that hearing her words in his head had. He allowed them to be there and change his perspective. He earned the medals for things he did that were good, not the things he did that were bad. Yes, people had died, but had he done nothing, everyone would have died. They'd lost people on the base, and he caused deaths on the enemy side doing what he did, and chances were some civilians, too, who were caught up in the fight that wasn't theirs. That didn't make it his fault.

"This is Warrant Officer Lucas Porter!" he yelled into the microphone. "The base is under attack! We need air support! Air support!" Another round of gunfire

tore through the station, and he dropped to the ground, his heart beating wildly in his chest. He looked left and right, knowing he was alone but hoping and praying he wasn't. Being alone meant being the one to make the decisions. Life and death decisions.

A firm headbutt to his thigh brought him back to the motel room. Haven was budging him, a whine low in his throat as he looked up at him with worried eyes. "I'm okay, boy," he promised, stroking his head until the dog sat back on his haunches. Haven didn't relax, but he didn't force him into the comfort position, either.

Lucas's gaze strayed to the bed again, and he lifted the fatigues, his fingers working at the Velcro on a patch that said PORTER until he could pull it off. The sound was soft but felt like ripping a bandage off an old wound. Sometimes, removing the bandage revealed a healed wound. He reached for the next patch, pulling that one off, too. Lucas held the patches in his hand, closed his eyes and did a mental search of his body for wounds. They were there. Some were healed. Some were closed over but still oozing. That told him he was getting somewhere. Slow as the healing was, he *was* healing.

The patches went into his pocket and the fatigues, dress blues and shoes were tucked into the bag. Before he put the medals away, he opened each box and ran his fingers over the object inside. "Earned for saving lives, not taking them," he uttered with each medal.

The one point they drove home at the VA in therapy was that he had to do the hard work if he wanted to be free of the guilt that plagued him. Would his mind ever heal from the horrific things he saw and participated in? No. Those scars would always remain, but if he could stop carrying some of the guilt and shame about them, his life would be better by default. He'd feel better physically and emotionally. Life still wouldn't be Skittles and rainbows, but it would be manageable again. He'd genuinely believed he'd done that, but seeing this bag again told him in no uncertain terms that he hadn't done anything at all.

His gaze strayed to the woman sitting at the desk, her concentration on the screen in front of her. She made him want to forget the guilt and shame he carried from those years long ago. Her honesty and openness about her struggles with PTSD made him feel less shame for having it, too. Her beliefs that he saved countless lives, including hers, made him want to set the guilt on a shelf somewhere and stop carrying it around in such a destructive way. There would always be triggers he'd have to work around. Those triggers were frequent and out of his control, and the reason he had Haven by his side. He had worked hard to protect himself and others by working with Haven, but now he understood the truth. He hadn't done the most demanding job of all. With his gaze pinned on Lilah's beautiful hair, he wondered if the episodes might be less frequent and less crushing each time they happened if he found a way to free himself of the shame and guilt. For the first time, he wanted to try.

Once the medals were back in the bag, he closed it and clicked the handle through the loops. The bag felt lighter when he carried it to the door and set it aside. Not just because he'd taken items out but because he did the hard work of taking back some of his power from it.

"You forgot the coat," Lilah said, and his head snapped up to meet her gaze. She was turned halfway in the chair and pointed at the bed with the field jacket spread across the end.

"I was thinking about keeping it out," he said, walking over to where she sat by the computer. "It was a new issue to me in Germany, but I never wore it but a couple of times. I noticed snowflakes earlier, and let's face it, that coat is warmer than anything we have with us. Seems smart to keep it handy, just in case."

"As long as you think you can," she said, her gaze pinned on him again.

As much as he wanted to talk to her about his feelings, he bit back the words on his tongue. They needed to concentrate on staying alive. "We have bigger problems on our hands right now, Lilah. Were you able to access the flash drive?"

After glancing at him, she turned back to the computer and clicked on the mouse pad. "I was. I've been familiarizing myself with it all again."

"These are the files that I was working on at the time of the attack," she explained, running the mouse down the screen, and he counted twelve files. She clicked the first one open. "I don't even know if these got shipped. As you can see," she explained, pointing out the different pieces of information on the screen, "I had just hit Send to get central shipping the routing information when the first missile hit." She closed her eyes with her breath held tightly in her chest. It had always been that way for her. Thinking about the first minutes of the attack. The confusion. The terror. All the things that go through your mind when you think you're about to die.

He gently massaged her back while Haven rested his

chin on her lap. "Open your eyes. You're not there any-more. You're with me again. I'll keep you safe."

Lilah opened her eyes and turned to meet his gaze. "Just like you did that day, Luca. I hate having to put you through that again. I hate that my presence here has put you in danger, but I can't change it, can I?"

"Nope," he said with a chuckle. "Embrace the suck, as they say, and remember that we did a lot of hard things as a team. We can do it again."

"Right," she said with a nod of her head and the clear-ing of her throat. "As I said, I don't know if central ship-ping got any of this."

"I thought Mina said they could see it all from a dif-ferent computer or something."

"That depends on if the email sent or was stopped by the missile attack. You know how the tech was over there. Also, I don't know if the relics were found on the base afterward."

"Wait, you mean these twelve were actually on the base? They weren't spread out across other bases?"

"That's what I'm saying. I was finishing the cata-log for a collection brought to us by a museum curator turned soldier. He wanted to protect the oldest relics of his collection."

"And then we go and lose them to history," Lucas said, whistling a low tune. "Doesn't look good on our end."

"Or his," she said, showing him the country of ori-gin. "It was his government that attacked us. The thing is, I don't know if they're lost to history or not. Those twelve are an unknown to me."

"Ha," Lucas said with a shake of his head. "Okay, I feel less bad about it now. Do you think they want this information because they found the relics? Maybe they want to get them back to the right people or need the paper trail to get them back home?"

"First, they don't know I have this drive with the information on it, so why wouldn't they simply send me official army orders to return to a base and give them whatever information I could remember? Why all the games and the attempts to take me against my will?" she asked, motioning at her chin. "It doesn't make sense."

She was right, it didn't make sense. None of it made sense. He stared at the computer screen and a folder caught his eye. He pointed at it. "What's that file?"

"That's a bit of a side project I was working on. It doesn't apply to these files." She motioned at the list before her.

"The Lost Key of Honor. It sounds important." He lifted a brow, and she sighed, bringing the cursor up but stopping before she clicked it open.

"I think it's important. Important enough that I'm not going to open this file and show you any part of it. What you don't know, you can't tell."

"I don't understand. Is it top secret or something?"

"I don't know what it is, Luca. Okay, I mean, I know what it is, but I don't know why there was so much subterfuge based around it."

"You mean they didn't assign you this file?" When she shook her head, he got a bad feeling in his gut. A feeling that said the file was TNT. "Show me."

"No," she said with another shake of her head. "The less you know about all of this, the better. It still gives you plausible deniability."

"It also makes it impossible for me to protect you,

Lilah. Plausible deniability is useless if you're dead or captured." His voice vibrated with all the fear bottled up in his gut. Haven walked over and sat next to him, leaning into his leg. Lucas found his head and stroked him, his gaze locked on the woman in the chair. Her face was drawn and drained of color, making the scars on her chin appear more prominent than ever before. Lucas traced the scar on her chin with his thumb, drawing a jagged breath from her lips. "You told me I had to trust you, so now I'm telling you the same thing. Trust me, Lilah, and we'll get through this."

Chapter Twelve

"You're sure?" she asked with a hard swallow punctuating the sentence. "Once you're involved, you're involved to the end."

"I'm already involved, Lilah," he reminded her, motioning at the room. "I've been involved since you walked out on me six years ago."

"That's not what I did, Luca! I was protecting you!" She shot up from her chair, but he grasped her upper arms to hold her in place. "I was protecting you," she whispered again, as though he hadn't heard her the first time.

"Which was honorable and, I'm sure, terribly difficult. I'm here now, and you've already involved me, so let me help you. If what you say about these guys is true, I can't go back to Secure One and carry on with my life as though the last few days didn't happen, right?" She shook her head, her lips in a thin line. "Then let me help you, really help you, end this situation so you can have your life back."

"You keep saying that, but if this ends and I'm still standing, I'm a woman with nothing. Now that's just as terrifying as facing down these guys."

"Now?" he asked, his thumb still tracing her chin.

Her heavy sigh said more as an answer than any words could have. She had relied on herself for so long that now, after finding him again, she found it difficult to walk away. He understood that sigh on a soul-deep level.

"You're sure you want to know all of this information?" she asked again, motioning at the computer. "We can't go back, so make sure you're prepared for what's to come."

"I'll be wading through what's to come with you whether I know or not, Lilah. I'm all in until you're safe. It's better to know what we're up against than fight an enemy without the knowledge needed to beat them."

Her curt nod and how she turned to the computer told him she accepted his decision. "This file refers to a trunk that a curator had brought in. It was a trunk they couldn't get open."

"He didn't bring the key along?"

"There is no key," she said, biting her lower lip. "The trunk is from ancient Iraq. It hasn't been opened for hundreds of years."

"The Lost Key of Honor," he said when the name struck him.

"Loosely translated," she agreed with a nod. "It was written in an old, dead language, but that was the best the curator could guess."

"He knew there was no key but wanted the trunk saved anyway?"

"There's a reason," she said, worrying her teeth across her lip as she clicked open the file. "It's been long believed that the trunk could hold—"

"The Holy Grail," he said with a breath as he pulled up a chair from the small table so he could sit. He took a moment to read the top paragraph of the file and let out a low whistle. "The trunk cannot be opened in any way other than with the key."

"There was little time to worry about it when it was brought in at the beginning of the war, so it was shipped to the States to be held at a museum."

"This file says they were actively looking for intel on the key. How did they expect to find a hundreds-year-old key in that kind of rubble when the country's own people couldn't find it?"

"Because it's not a key," she said, facing him. "It's a piece of a stone tablet. The museum has long had half of the tablet that fits into the top of the trunk. The word *grail* is written several times on that half of the tablet. Without the other half, they can't translate the entire tablet or open the trunk."

"Okay, but grail can just mean something sought after, too. That doesn't mean it's the Holy Grail, and why would it be in Iraq?"

"The four rivers of Eden are said to converge in southern Mesopotamia, which we know is modern-day Iraq. How it got there or why, I can't say, but as you can see, they have put together a strong argument for it being the Holy Grail. If you believe in all of that, of course."

"You don't?" Lucas asked, holding her gaze for a heartbeat before dragging it away to read the file. The information on the drive was extensive and would take more than a cursory glance to understand it all. He didn't have that kind of time, so he would have to depend on her to give him the highlights.

"I believe that others believe it to be true, Luca. Regardless of what is inside the trunk, the trunk itself is a relic and should be preserved. It could be empty, but it existed at that time for a reason. I never saw it in person. It was sent off the base before I arrived. I've only seen the images in the file."

"How do you have the file if you weren't in charge of the trunk?"

"It wasn't meant for my eyes, but I didn't know that then. I found it on a flash drive still in a computer on the base. I didn't know who the flash drive belonged to, but it was the only file on it. I may have transferred the file to my drive before I turned in the original."

"Why?"

"It intrigued me—The Lost Key of Honor. It drew me in and made me want to find it. I was intrigued by the question, where is it, and how could it even exist hundreds of years later?"

"It can't exist," he said with assuredness. "Not anymore. That country has been bombed and destroyed to the point no stone tablet from that time would ever be anything but dust."

"Unless it was protected somewhere," she said with a lift of one brow.

"Protected?"

After scrolling with the mouse several times, she pointed at the screen. "This picture shows the trunk with the half tablet in place. What do you notice?"

Once she enlarged the image so he could see it better, he stared for quite some time before pointing at a ridge. "There. Why would a ridge be in the center if it was one tablet? It's more like there are two separate tablets."

"Exactly," she said, a grin on her face. "Do you see the complicated notches on the side without the tablet?"

"All the indents?" he asked, and she nodded. "That's the key to opening it?"

"Best I can figure," she agreed. "The file indicates that several molds were made in an attempt to make a new key for it, but they all failed to open it."

"Strange. I'm surprised someone hasn't just busted the trunk apart by now. Why continue to search for something likely long gone?"

"Human nature? Spiritual beliefs? Fear?"

"Fear?" Lucas asked, holding her gaze, wholly engaged in the conversation even as he kept his ears open to the noises outside the motel. Cars speeding past on the highway. Tires at an even speed, not slowing or turning. No footsteps crunching across the snow. All was quiet.

"Fear of what might happen if they break the trunk to get it open. What does the other half of the tablet say? Is it a curse to open it without certain people present? That kind of thing. If people think this trunk holds the Holy Grail, they would never destroy it to get it open."

"Okay, I get that, but we both know that the other half of the tablet is long gone. Even if it's not, if the people of Iraq can't find it, how could we as foreigners?"

"I don't have the answer to that, only that they were trying."

"As a good faith mission for Iraq or…?"

"Again, I don't have the answer to that. I don't know who started this file or sanctioned the search. It's been six years. For all I know, the trunk has been returned and none of it matters now. I've been running for six years from some unknown enemy who wants me dead, and I don't know why! I just want to know what's going on!"

On instinct, he pulled her into him and held her

tightly. "It's okay," he promised, soothing her by rocking her gently. "I know you're stressed, scared and exhausted. You're not alone anymore, and we might not be able to solve this in one night, but you have help now."

Lucas fell silent, rubbing her back as he held her, letting her rest her chin over his shoulder, heavy with fatigue. It was time for her to get some sleep, but he would be selfish a bit longer and continue to languish in the feel of her wrapped around him. He'd missed her warmth and how she made him feel safe in an unsafe world. Now it was his turn to do that for her, and he would. First, she needed someone to take care of her. He was grateful to be the one to get that chance again.

"Come on," he said, hoisting her from the chair and helping her to the bed. "It's time to let your mind rest and your body recover. You're exhausted. You need to sleep in a bed where you can stretch out and recoup."

Lilah didn't argue. Instead, she lowered herself to the bed and let him remove her boots before she slid her legs under the covers. "You're safe here tonight," he promised, pulling her spectacles off her face and setting them on the nightstand. That was a blanket statement he shouldn't be promising, but he willed it to be true. "I'm going to contact the team and stand watch."

"Just a few hours," she murmured, her eyes drooping as he stroked her forehead. It was an old trick he used to use when she refused to sleep that summer, worried he'd do something terrible to himself while she did.

"I'll wake you in two hours," he promised, but he wouldn't. He'd let her sleep in the safety of another human being for as long as he could. While Lilah slept, he hoped Mina would find something they could use to move this investigation forward and get the target off her back. They'd already been shot at twice. As he lowered himself to the computer and minimized the file that might hold the answer to everything, the only thought running through his head was, the third time was the charm.

Chapter Thirteen

"Lilah, wake up." She opened her eyes to see Lucas looming over her. "Time to go."

Without question, she sat up and tied on her boots. "Did they find us already?" she asked, slipping her glasses onto her face again.

"Hard to know, but Cal reported that someone is sniffing around the vicinity of the medal. He wants us to move again to be on the safe side."

The room was dark as she stood from the bed and took in her surroundings. He'd packed up all the equipment, and the bags sat ready by the door. He handed her his Secure One parka, the sleeves already rolled up.

"Here, put this on. I know it's a bit too big, but it's snowing now, and if we go off the road, you need something warmer than the coat Mina gave you."

"What about you?" she asked, slipping her arms into the coat that was, in fact, a bit too big, but with the sleeves rolled up, it would be wearable and keep her legs warm, too.

He slid into his field coat and buttoned it up. "We might as well use it to our advantage, right?" His tone told her he needed her to agree.

"Right," she said, grabbing the front of it and planting a kiss on his cheek. "I'm proud of you, Luca."

His smile told her she'd given him the answer he needed. "Wait here. I'll take the bags to the van and see what I see."

After her nod, he turned to Haven, already dressed for the weather. "Rest, Haven. Stay with Lilah." As though the dog understood the assignment, he walked over and sat, his ears at attention. "Good boy."

Lilah wanted to reach down and scratch his ears, but she knew better than to touch any service dog while they were working. Instead, she motioned for Luca to go and stepped back so she wasn't visible when he opened the door. Watching through the window, he threw the bags where they could reach them quickly and then checked for anyone on the road before he pulled off the magnet on the side of the van and switched it out.

"Get ready, boy," she said to Haven. "It's going to be cold."

She pulled the hood up on the parka and was ready when he opened the door. "Haven, fall in." The dog headed straight for the open van door while Luca helped her out of the motel and into the passenger seat. "Buckle up," he said, shutting the door for her before he secured Haven and slammed the side door.

Once they were on the move, she glanced over at him. "Where are we headed?"

"Somewhere southwest. Mina says we're supposed to drive out of the snow quickly. I hope she's right. The conditions aren't great."

Lilah tried to see through the falling snow, but it was nearly impossible in the dark, even with the windshield wipers on high. "Try the conditions are terrible, and no plows will be out way up here."

"The only upside is we have the road to ourselves. If nothing else, it will be a white Christmas."

"I can't argue with you there." After a glance in the side mirror, she started to chuckle. "Larry's Computer Repair. If we can't fix it, it ain't broke," she read from the sign on the side of the van. "Really?"

Luca wore a grin when she glanced back at him. "What can I say? Cal has a sense of humor. It's not much in the way of camouflage, but it does say something different than the last one, which was pizza delivery. With a little snow packed on the license plate, no one will know it's us immediately."

"You said Cal has eyes on someone stalking the medal?" She hadn't wanted to ask the question, but at the same time, she wanted to know the answer.

"That's what his eyes in the sky say, but he's waiting it out to see if they're just in the area or specifically searching for something."

"Or someone. I can't believe you might be right about this," she said, chewing on her lip. "It never occurred to me, mostly because I can't believe they could be tracking me with something so small for so long."

"Technology has evolved, Lilah. They make trackers now that only use power when they're pinged. The rest of the time, they're off. These small military trackers only use solar power to charge them, so it wouldn't take much time out of your pocket each month to keep it charged. For instance, having it out on a dresser for a day would give it charge for months."

"But why?" she asked, her hand grasping the door

handle as the wheels slid toward the shoulder of the road. He got it under control again just before hitting the rumble strips, wherever they may be under the snow.

"I think we both know why," he said, tightly gripping the wheel. "They want to know where you are at all times. They may not know about the flash drive, but you exist, and you know things about what went down there."

Lilah fell silent as she watched the wipers clear the glass and the snow cover it again in a comforting pattern. She did know things. Things she wished she didn't and things she wished she knew about now that she was faced with people hunting her. She rubbed her chin absently as though that would make the jagged scar disappear. A thought struck her, and she gasped, the sound loud in the quiet van.

"What if I didn't even earn the medal and they just gave it to me to keep track of me?" To her ears, the sentence was incredulous but also wholly possible.

"No," Luca said, shaking his head as he steered the van around a sharp corner. They were doing barely twenty in a fifty-five, but until this snow quit, they were at its mercy. "Don't think like that. We don't even know if it is the medal. It's just a hypothesis right now."

"But you said Cal has seen activity around it."

"I also said he's waiting to see if it's approached, so just give him time to get back to me."

"What else did Mina say?"

"She's looking into the news archives about antiquities or tablets discovered or displayed over the last six years. She's also trying to get more information about the accusations against Major Burris."

"Something is fishy there," Lilah agreed. "The major

was always professional and was scarily knowledge-able about the laws and customs that applied in armed conflicts."

"Even knowledgeable men have a price, Lilah."

She fell silent for several more minutes as she thought about Burris. Was he the kind of man who willingly stole precious artifacts for money? Not the man she'd worked under, but then again, everyone has a face they show the world and a face that hides below. She had to wonder if the face Burris hid was one of corruption and theft. "I hope she finds something helpful. Tell me how you started working at Secure One," she said to change the subject.

Luca's chuckle was self-deprecating if she'd ever heard it. "When I left the training program with Haven, my first job was working security for Senator Dorian in Minneapolis. Secure One worked an on-site event for the senator's daughter during the Red River Slayer's reign. Do you remember that?"

"Of course," she said with a nod. "That was a terrifying time for women around the country. It was hard to believe when the whole story came out."

"Truth. While Secure One was at the estate, I helped them protect the property's perimeter when the senator's daughter was at risk. Once the case was wrapped up and Secure One went home, Cal reached out and thanked me for helping them with everything. I replied that if there were ever any openings on his team, I would love to interview, with his understanding that it was two for the price of one," he explained, his gaze flicking to the rearview mirror to check on his dog. "He had me drive up within days, and I was hired on the spot. They had so much work coming in after being in the public eye so often over the previous years with high-profile cases that they were turning down jobs."

"That's fabulous to hear, Luca," she said, touching his arm as he drove. "I'm glad you took the chance and asked."

"I almost didn't," he admitted with a tip of his head. "High-stress situations were always difficult for me after we returned, but I'd worked for the senator for three years without problems. Not that it was high stress, other than Senator Dorian loved nothing more than to yell about everything that went on across the property, right or wrong. My therapy from the VA and training with Haven was put to the test during those few days that the property was locked down, and I was able to handle it without difficulty. That was the only reason I inquired about working at Secure One. Well, that and the fact that his core team was all ex-military and understood the ups and downs of PTSD."

"Mina indicated that was the case to me, too," she agreed. "Understanding helps, but so does having a brotherhood again, right?"

"At first, I thought that might work against me," he admitted, letting the van pick up speed a bit more now that the snow had turned to just flurries. "I was afraid the environment would remind me too much of my military years, but I quickly saw that wasn't how Cal ran the business. He was a participant in the company and not the boss. It all works, despite our different experiences and reactions to them."

"No, it works *because* of your different experiences and reactions to them," she clarified. "You all bring different perspectives and knowledge to the table about different aspects of the security world. That's what makes it work. You're an expert at weapons but need a sharpshooter like Efren to use your knowledge practically."

"You know Efren was a sharpshooter?" She noticed the quizzical look he wore when he asked the question.

"Mina gave me a bit of a rundown on everyone as I was changing clothes," she explained. "She didn't want me walking into a meeting completely uninformed."

"That sounds like Mina," Luca said with a chuckle. "She's always about keeping the playing field level, which is funny coming from her."

"Why?"

"Mina is the smartest person in the company, male or female, and we all know it. None of us can do what she can with a computer and a few hours on her side. Before Mina joined the team, from what they tell me, they were nothing more than glorified security camera installers. Cal was doing work on the side to fund the company."

"What kind of work on the side?"

Luca cleared his throat and kept his eyes straight ahead. "Let's just say he did many things he didn't want to do to help good people who were suffering."

Her military experience translated that statement quickly into one word. Mercenary. "Understood."

"Now that Mina is part of the team, the business has grown, so Cal is starting a cybersecurity division. Mina will be heading it up. I foresee it quickly overtaking the personal security aspect of the business."

"There will be no doubt," she said, noticing a sign pointing them back toward Whiplash, Minnesota. Secure One was located on the town's southern border, but they wouldn't go there again until her situation was cleared up. Then again, she'd probably never return to Secure One, no matter how much she wanted to. "I worked remotely for a company for three of the six years I was on the run. My job was to keep their server safe, build their website utilizing hidden pages and code everything into a box. If anyone tried to brick their system, mine would do it first, allowing me to unbrick it again once the hackers were caught."

He glanced at her quickly before putting his eyes back on the road. "You can do that?"

"I could, back then," she agreed. "It was difficult work but worth it. These days, those techniques may not work anymore."

"It couldn't have been that long ago, Lilah. You were only gone six years."

"I quit three years ago, and things change at lightning speed in the tech world."

"Why did you quit?"

"I didn't see any other choice when they found me for the fourth time in three years. My only hope was to go completely underground and stay off their radar. Little did I know I may have been carrying that radar with me. Anyway, I banked a lot of money during the years I worked, and since it was remote work, it didn't matter if I had to move to a different town. I saved every penny I could over the years by living in some disgusting places, but it paid off. I survived on what I had for years and only needed to do odd jobs here and there to keep myself fed and clothed. I've spent so long on the run, I'm not sure I know how to stay in one place anymore."

"It's easy," he said with his lips quirked. "You find someplace that feels like home and you stay there."

"Easy coming from your side of the van, yes," she agreed, leaning her head on the cool glass of the window. "Not so easy when where you feel at home is off-limits."

"Where do you feel at home?"

"I've only ever felt at home with you, Luca."

Chapter Fourteen

I've only ever felt at home with you, Luca.

Try as he might, he couldn't get those words out of his head. Her sweet voice telling him how she felt even when she couldn't tell him how she felt made him want to stop the van and drag her across the console to finish that kiss from the motel room. He knew better. Whatever had stopped her last time was still between them, and while he wished he knew what it was, all he could do was let her reveal it in her own time.

Those words had kept him alert and awake on a long drive through bad weather. He wanted to keep her safe, so he'd driven as long as he could before fatigue set in. They'd found another small motel and pulled over for the night, knowing if he didn't, they wouldn't see morning.

"Secure one, Whiskey," the voice said, and Lucas hit the microphone button to connect.

"Secure two, Lima."

Mina's face filled the screen, and she immediately assessed the room around them. "You're safe?"

"For now," he said with a nod. "We're in a new motel south of the Minnesota border. We didn't pick up any tails, and all's quiet on the western front."

"Do you have enough supplies?" Cal's voice asked from off in the distance. Mina zoomed the screen out and included the rest of the room in the shot. Cal and Roman were there with her.

"We stopped and picked up food at a small grocery on the way down the hill."

"Wearing Secure One gear?" Mina asked with her lips in a thin line.

"No, I, uh, actually wore my field coat. Found it in my duffel and thought it would be good cover." All three sets of brows went up, but they said nothing, so he cleared his throat. "Would you thank Sadie for dumping that giant bag of food in the back for Haven? It's less stressful when I don't worry about him."

"You know she's got her little dude," Mina said with a wink.

Lilah laughed, and he sat silently until the sound died away, soaking it up in case he never heard it again. "Have you learned anything since we last talked?"

"Yes," Cal and Mina said in unison, but Mina motioned for him to go first.

Cal spun his computer screen around to face the camera in the conference room. "We've been monitoring the house where I put the medal. It's an old abandoned place north of town and within a thirty-minute walk of the storage units."

"To make it look like I escaped and took shelter there?" Lilah asked.

"Exactly. I did it because you wouldn't stay there long if you were with us. They would need to move quickly to get another team there."

"Or there was already another team waiting."

Cal pointed at her and nodded. "I believe that's the case. As you'll see." He hit a button on the computer, and they watched as four men approached the house with their rifles raised.

"Are those AR-15s?" Lucas asked immediately.

"No, M4 Carbine EPRs," Cal answered.

"I thought M4 Carbines were for military only," Delilah said.

"These are law enforcement guns. The ERP stands for an enhanced patrol rifle. Better sights. Better stock. There's more room for mounting optics and accessories. The guys at the storage unit debacle had the same ones," Cal said, his face wearing a grim expression.

"That's odd because an AR-15 is much cheaper these days. If you're a gun for hire, you're carrying an AR-15, not an M4," Lucas said, confused by the whole thing.

"Unless someone is buying them for you," Lilah whispered. They all went silent as the four men left the house like ninjas in the night. "Do you think they found the medal?" she asked, gazing at the screen. Lucas could hear how much courage it took her to ask.

"No. It's inaccessible to them, but it will have to remain there for now," Cal said.

"Either way, they know we're on to them," Lucas said, reaching over and squeezing Lilah's hand. She held on for dear life, so he didn't let go. Instead, he ran his thumb over her hand to keep her calm.

"How did you even get that footage?" Lilah asked, her head cocked as though the thought just struck her.

"Drone in a tree," Cal explained. "Easier and faster than putting up a camera when your timeline is short."

"Okay, we know they're still looking for Lilah," Lucas

said, getting them back on track. "We also know some of them are ex-military or law enforcement. Mina, did you find out anything?"

"So many things," Mina said with laughter on her lips. It brought a smile to his, and he glanced at Lilah to see her wearing one, too. Leave it to Mina to keep the moment light.

"I did some digging into Major Burris. He was never tried for the war crimes he was accused of because, according to JAG, the case was weak, with little evidence. However, he was within a year of retirement, so he served it at a desk and was ushered out on his last day."

"I bet he was," Lilah murmured. "I would love to know who brought those charges against him. Burris was always professional and the person we could go to when we had an issue. It seems off for his level of command and his personality."

"War does funny things to people," Mina gently said. "Kindness to his people doesn't mean he was kind to the enemy."

"That's true, I know," Lilah agreed. "I would just like to find out who was at the heart of those charges."

"Burris is now living near Rochester, Minnesota. I'll see if I can dig deeper and find more information about his accusers," Mina said, making a note. "Colonel Swenson is still working but is now a general in Minneapolis."

"Not surprised," Lucas said. "I worked a few ops with him, and he was voted most likely to be in the army for his career. He lived for the accolades and back patting he got moving up the ranks. He went into a funk if someone didn't tell him how wonderful he was every day. We used to call him Major Payne and Captain Fantastic."

Cal snorted while biting back a smile, but Lucas saw it. There wasn't a guy who had served who didn't know someone like Swenson.

"You'll find a lot of that kind of guy in the military," Roman said, still chuckling. "I guess that's one of the reasons we have career army men. They thrive in that environment. Anything else, Mina?"

"Yes," she said, leaning in on the table to address Lucas personally. "I called about that trunk you asked me to check on. The museum doesn't have and never has had a trunk like you described."

"What?" Lilah asked in surprise. "I have documented paperwork that it went to them."

"Not according to the museum curator who I spoke with there. He said they are sometimes sent to a different museum during shipping because one may have more room. I haven't had time to call other museums, nor would I know where to start."

Lilah cut her gaze to Lucas for a moment, and he recognized the look. She wasn't convinced that Mina was right. "I'll take care of it," Lilah said before Mina could say more. "As long as I can use the Secure One computer for a little questionable hacking?"

"As long as you're only looking," Cal said with a brow raised.

"Look, but don't touch. Got it," Lilah said with a wink.

"We can split the list if you send me the information," Mina said, elbows on the table. "I'm at your disposal."

When Lilah shot a look Lucas's way, he read in it that she wanted no one else involved more than they had to be. "It's no problem. I can do the museums while you keep looking into Burris's accusers?"

"Sure," Mina said. "I'm just worried you're both running on little to no sleep."

"I got to sleep last night while Lucas drove. He can sleep while I work."

"No," Lucas said immediately and without hesitation. "Someone has to be on watch. We can assume the medal was their dowsing rod, but we can't be sure. We can't let our guard down."

"You also can't go without sleep," Cal said, his words pointed. "Everyone in this room knows what happens when we push ourselves past the brink of exhaustion."

"I can keep watch and do the work," Lilah said, emphasizing her sentence by squeezing his hand no one else knew she was holding. "We're a team, and I can carry my weight on it."

Cal pointed at the computer screen. "What she said. We'll let you get to it. It's 6:00 a.m. now. The next check-in will be at noon unless something imperative arises. If you need backup, you know how to reach us. I still have the van monitored, so I know your exact location. You should be good for the day as the snow is about to hit your area and no one will move anywhere until it passes."

"Tell me about it," Lucas muttered. "Driving down from the North Shore last night was one of the most dangerous things I've done, and I worked munitions."

"You don't mess with Mother Nature," Roman said. "Take advantage of the break. Hopefully, by the time the snow passes, Min and Delilah will have what you need to take the next step."

"Charlie, out," Cal said, and the screen went blank.

Lucas turned to Lilah and took her other hand. "Why wouldn't the museum have the trunk?"

"That's what I want to know, too," she agreed.

"Can it just happen that a shipment is diverted?"

"Not unless the museum it's going to has burned down and closed. Then it would just get returned to sender, essentially, and routed back to central shipping. All of these antiquities have well-documented shipping papers for a reason. We never want to be accused of stealing other countries' precious art or artifacts."

"Maybe it did get returned to sender and sent somewhere else? There would be no way for you to know once we left the base."

"Except that the trunk was shipped before I got to the base, remember? I have images of that trunk in a museum in The Lost Key of Honor file."

"Are you sure it's a museum?" he asked, his brow raised.

She paused and tipped her head, probably thinking about the pictures she'd seen. "No, I can't be sure. I'll go through the images and inspect them closer."

"If it was at a museum, how would you track it down? Mina is right. There are a lot of museums."

"I'm going to do it the easy way."

"The easy way? Only contacting the museums you know took in antiquities during that time of the war?"

"No," she said, turning to the computer and inserting the flash drive. "I'll start by looking for the first six I sent out when I arrived. I know those left the base."

"To what end?"

"It's a first step. I'll know if some of the artifacts made it to their destination or if none of them did. It's a place to start while you sleep."

"No. I'm not leaving you without protection."

"If you don't sleep, you'll be useless to me if we need to run, Luca. Cal is right. Exhaustion makes everything worse, and I need you to be able to think on your feet. Look, the snow has already started." She moved the curtain aside so he could see the flakes falling. "No one is going anywhere, including us."

His shoulders slumped in defeat. "Only a few hours. Wake me the moment you think you hear something. I mean it, Lilah. It's easier to be proactive in these situations than reactive."

"On my honor, I will wake you at the wisp of a worry that there's trouble."

She stood and held his hand as she walked him to the bed. The motel only had rooms with one queen, and they'd taken it, but he had seen how her eyes grew when they walked in. She was hiding something he was determined to figure out. Once he had laid down on the bed, boots on, she covered him with a blanket and turned off the light. It was early and the sun wasn't up yet, but the way the storm was howling, he doubted they'd see much daylight over the next twelve hours.

Lilah kissed his cheek and lingered as though she were fighting a war with herself before she walked back to the desk to sit. Lucas fell asleep to the backdrop of her keys clacking as she set about her work. He couldn't help but wonder if the secrets were really hidden within that file or if they had been hidden in her all along.

Chapter Fifteen

Confusion and frustration filled Lilah as she stared at the screen. She had been working her way down the list of the dozens of shipping logs for the antiquities she had on the flash drive. She was nine deep, and so far, none of them had found their way to where they were supposed to be. In fact, it was as though they had just disappeared into thin air.

Lilah started typing again, trying to cross match the item across museums in case the schedule got screwed up when the base fell. Maybe one didn't reach the intended place but went to the museum where a different artifact was scheduled. Her fingers paused on the keyboard. If that were the case, they would have been returned to central shipping. It didn't make sense. She had no other ideas, so she tried it anyway, just in case museums were told to keep the item rather than return it.

After another hour of digging, it was easy to see that the theory was also incorrect. How was it that all these items had gone poof into thin air? The antiquities she was searching for weren't even on the base when it fell, so there would be no reason to think they didn't get shipped correctly.

Her neck and back aching, she stood and stretched, her shirt pulling up to reveal what she was trying to hide from the man sleeping on the bed behind her. She quickly pulled her shirt down and tucked it back into her pants. She had been working for nearly five hours, meaning Lucas had been sleeping for as long. Everything was quiet, and she was confident they'd have until the snow stopped before they had to worry about being on guard. Then again, if the medal had been to blame for leading these guys to her door, it would be much more difficult for them to find her now.

The idea that they took something she had pride in and turned it against her made her sick to her stomach. Had she earned the medal or was it just how they decided to keep track of her? That was risky, considering she could have done what Lucas did and stored the medal. Her mind drifted back to some of her conversations with other soldiers. She had said more than once that if given a medal, she would carry it with her always as a reminder that she could do hard things. Someone could have easily overheard her and used that statement to their advantage.

Now, here she was, six years of her life gone. Six years she didn't get to spend with the man sleeping behind her because someone played her strength as her weakness. Ironic. None of it made sense, though. Why would the government want or need to track her?

"Hey," Lucas said, sitting up and stretching. "How long have I been out?"

"Almost five hours," she said, the room nearly dark even in the middle of the day. The snow was falling so hard it felt like night rather than morning. "Feel better?"

"Much," he admitted. "That drive wore me out last night. Everything quiet?"

"As a church mouse. No one is out in this. You can't see your hand in front of your face. Why don't you take a shower?"

"No," he said, shaking his head at the suggestion. "Vulnerability could get you killed."

Her sigh was heavy when she stood to face him. "I'm capable of taking care of myself, Lucas Porter. I took Haven outside to do his business while you were sleeping and look, we're both fine."

"You did what? Why didn't you wake me up? You shouldn't have gone out there!"

"I was trained by the United States Army and kept myself alive through attack after attack for the last six years. I have a gun and know how to use it. Stop acting like my bodyguard and start acting like my partner." She tapped his chest with each syllable to drive her point home.

She didn't miss his small step back as he raised his brows. "Your partner?"

"We always made great partners, Lucas. No matter what we were doing, we played to each other's strengths and weaknesses without the need to communicate them. It was that way from when you picked me up off the tarmac and we pushed that old golf cart out of our way. I know it's been years, but you can trust me to have your back."

The look in his eye told her he remembered when they were partners in crime *and* between the bedsheets. "I'll be out in a few. The rifle is by the door if you need it."

Her salute was jaunty, bringing a smile to his lips for

the first time since he woke up. "When you get out, I'll share what I learned while you slept."

After grabbing his bag and giving her a nod, he jogged into the small bathroom and closed the door. Lilah lowered herself to the chair and wondered if the Luca she used to know was still under those black fatigues or if he had become someone completely different since their summer on the island. Spending time with him the last few days told her that he was someone completely different from everyone but her. He had a hard edge to him now that he had never carried before, but maybe that was how he managed his emotions in the workplace and kept himself grounded during high-stress events. He was never sharp with her, and when their eyes met, it was as though the last six years had been stripped away. That was when she saw the same vulnerable, scared, resilient man before her.

Lifting her shirt, she ran her hand over her belly, the scarred ridges of puckered flesh under her fingers a reminder of how she had changed. When she stripped her clothes off, she was no longer the same woman he remembered. She was alive but dead inside, her heart only beating at the thought of, or the sight of, the man in the shower. Even though she knew she couldn't be with him again, a tiny piece of her heart wanted that chance. A second chance at a fleeting love of youthful innocence. It wasn't youthful innocence, though. It was a shared understanding of a shared experience that shaped who they would become. The love wasn't fleeting, either. It was still there. She could feel it every time they touched, but it was a different kind of love now. Instead of a roaring flame of desire, it was a barely-there ember that could remember what they had together but could never flare strong enough to start that fire again.

Lilah shook her head and sighed, rubbing her face while she tried to refocus on the things she learned during her search. She had sent Mina a message asking if she had more information about the charges against Burris, but she hadn't replied yet. It had only been a few hours, but she was anxious to make some part of this complicated, frustrated puzzle fit together. She had purposely not mentioned what she found to Mina, hoping that Lucas could help her understand it before relaying the information to the team.

When she heard Lucas rustling about in the bathroom to dress, she made him a cup of coffee from the single cup maker on the counter and handed it to him when he came out.

"Thanks," he said, lifting it in the air. "Did you track down the trunk?"

He lowered himself to the end of the bed to sit opposite her while they talked. She liked how he was always dialed in on her and was never distracted by outside factors. She could tell he had a firm handle on everything outside the motel, which was very quiet right now.

"I didn't track it down. It's nowhere to be found, but that's not all," Delilah said, spinning in her chair and showing him how she had made a spreadsheet as she cross-referenced all the items she couldn't find.

"Wait, all of them are missing?"

"Missing in the respect that I can't find any of them in the places I sent them or even as being checked into a museum. My original thought was maybe they got the wrong shipping labels put on, so I looked for each one at each of the six museums, but there was nothing."

"How is that possible?"

"That's what I've been asking myself for hours. I'll keep checking the remaining items, but I feel squishy inside."

"Squishy?" he asked, his head tipped to the side in confusion.

"That two plus two doesn't equal four in this case. Squishy in my gut, wondering if I blindly participated in something I shouldn't have."

"You were following orders, Lilah. Don't take whatever this is on your shoulders. Can you tell me first why these items needed to be protected and second why they would disappear?"

"No," she said with a shake of her head. "Well, I know they were being protected from theft or destruction from war. Why they'd disappear is anyone's guess. They may not have disappeared. They could be in a warehouse somewhere. All I can do is follow the paper trail that leads me nowhere."

"It's been six years. Maybe they were returned to their respective countries already?"

"I would say that's possible if there was any evidence that they had been checked into a museum and back out again. We don't have that evidence, and like anything in the military, it should be there with bells on."

"True," he agreed, his hands massaging her shoulders as he stood over her chair to read the screen. He worked at the knotted muscles that were the consequences of too much time hunched over the laptop, stress and too many years away. But with his hands on her again, she melted under the familiarity of his touch. "Did Mina find anything while I was asleep?"

"I messaged her but haven't heard back." An idea came to her, and she glanced up at him. "I just thought of something!"

Her fingers flew across the keyboard until a website popped up.

"The Smithsonian?" he asked, his hands pausing on her shoulders.

"They were going to host one of the full exhibits we sent over."

"Six years ago, darling," he said in that familiar drawl that sent her right back to the first time they met. He'd driven her to the cafeteria where they'd had lunch together. When it was time to part, he'd said, "If I never see you again, I want you to know I think you're darling. A bright spot in a place where there are few to go around and little is charming. I do hope to see you again, my darling Delilah." I guess that was the moment she'd become smitten with Warrant Officer Porter.

"Right, and I don't expect them to still have the exhibit open, but their archives are open to the public to search. Since I have the names of those exhibits on the flash drive, it's easy to see if they were ever on display at the museum."

She typed the name of one of the exhibits into the search box, changing spellings and the order of the words every way she could to get a hit, but nothing came up, no matter what she typed in. He continued to massage her shoulders, which relaxed her and keyed her up simultaneously. Being with this man again was hard enough, but having his hands on her and knowing she couldn't have him was torture.

"There's nothing here."

"I'm starting to share your squishy feeling," he said, gazing at the screen. "Something should have come up, right?"

"Many somethings," she agreed, facing him to break the connection between his hands and her body.

Delilah stood and started pacing, trying to think of other ways to search for these exhibits. There were so many museums they could have gone to if they'd been routed wrong, but after all these years, it was anyone's guess where.

"There you go, buddy," Lucas said, lowering himself to the bed again after he put food in Haven's bowl. "We slept through breakfast." The dog tucked into the bowl, crunching kibble as she continued to pace. "The question is, why were none of these things put on exhibit if that was why they were sent here?"

She tapped her chin and stared at the window, the ugly, brown floral curtains blocking the snow and the daylight from the room. She was wrapped in a cocoon of safety that she knew would dissipate when she stepped out those doors. Someone was still after her, and she needed to figure out why.

"No!" she exclaimed as her heart started to pound. "The question isn't why weren't they on exhibit."

Luca was leaning back on the bed, braced on both hands, when he glanced up at her. "Okay, what is the question then?"

"The question is and always has been, why do they keep trying to kill me?"

In one fluid motion, Lucas stood in front of her. "Kill you? I thought they were trying to take you against your will."

"In the beginning," she agreed, intimidated by his stance before her. As she gazed into his eyes, she accepted it wasn't intimidation. It was protection. He would take a bullet for her before he let her get hurt. She leaned into his chest with her fist and forearm, the memories of the last few days hitting her square in the chest. "You might remember that the last few attempts have been all bullets and no brawn."

Instinctively, he grasped the fist she had against his chest and held it there. "We haven't stopped moving long enough for me to consider that, but you're right. They weren't trying to take you hostage. They were trying to kill you."

"The last time they found me, right before I sent you the message, they came in guns blazing, too. I think they shot my neighbor." Her eyes closed, and her voice broke on the last word. "That's on me."

"No," he said, tenderly kissing her forehead. "That's on the guy with the gun and no one else. He didn't need to shoot your neighbor. He chose to shoot your neighbor. You can't blame yourself for anything that's happened over the years since we were discharged."

"I do, though. I made choices that had ripples of consequences both for me and the people around me without them even knowing."

"What dictated those choices?"

She leaned her head against his chest to avoid his gaze. "The people after me. The alerts that I'd been found. The fear that filled me all day, every day."

"The people after you. That's who is responsible for any fallout around us, Lilah. I think it's time to go back to the beginning if we want to sort this out."

"Back to the beginning?" she asked, lifting her head.

"To the first time you were attacked. I want to know everything day by day, year by year, until we met up again on that island."

"Luca, that would take all day."

His hands went out to his sides to motion around the room. "We have no place to be. In fact, we have nowhere to go until we come up with some reason why ex-military hitmen keep knocking on your door, so let's do our due diligence now in the hopes that a week from now, you'll have your life back."

She held his gaze, read his thoughts and understood his frustrations. There was more in those chocolate eyes than determination and frustration, though. There was desire. A heat she knew all too well. A need left unfulfilled for too long. Her reckoning was coming, but she had an ace in the hole that would squelch that desire and extinguish the ember once and for all. She just had to be strong enough to play it.

Chapter Sixteen

Lucas listened to Lilah walk him step-by-step through the horrifying events she'd lived through over the last six years. Delilah was stronger than anyone he'd ever known, and he let her slip through his fingers. The moment she didn't show up to visit at the hospital as promised, he should have checked himself out and gone after her before her trail went cold. Instead, he let his past abandonment issues with his mother color the situation. He let his pain and his pride prevent him from tearing apart the entire country to find her.

"Why did I allow this to happen to you?" he muttered when she turned from the makeshift whiteboard they'd made with paper on the motel wall.

"Luca, you didn't allow anything. You had no control over it."

"I had control over what I did the moment you didn't come back to visit me. I had control over the way I let my hurt and embarrassment at being discarded by another woman I loved consume me. I should have stopped to remember the Delilah Hartman I knew. That woman always kept her promises. If I had looked at it in the proper light, I would have realized that you didn't abandon me.

No, that's what I did to you!" he exclaimed, his finger jabbing himself in the chest.

Lilah laid the marker down on the desk and walked to him, slipping her arms around his waist to rest her head on his chest. The memories hit him from the early days, but when he gazed down at her, the reality of the situation was evident in the jagged scars across her chin.

"You have to stop, Luca. I would have thought the same if I had been in your shoes. This isn't about who did the right or the wrong thing. This situation is about circumstances neither of us controlled, okay?"

Rather than agree or disagree, he held her, his chin resting on her head as he swallowed every bit of her warmth and comfort. His gaze was pinned on the wall of information that she'd been writing down, searching for any pattern or clue as to who was terrorizing her and why.

"What does 'The Mask' mean?" he asked, looking at the four events she'd written the words next to, including one just a few weeks ago.

She stepped out of his arms, and while he mourned the loss of her heat, he had finally found a pattern. He walked to the board and pointed to the four dates. The first was the night she'd dropped him at the hospital. The second was several years later, the third was about ten months ago and the final one was the night her neighbor had been shot.

"Those are the times I was approached by the guy I call 'The Mask.' He wore one of those extremely cold weather military masks."

"The ones that cover the nose and mouth and only leave the eyes uncovered?"

"Creepy as all get-out up close on a dark street," she said, a shudder going through her. "He covered his eyes with reflective sunglasses or goggles, which made it more terrifying. You could see your reflection in the lenses. You were a witness to your own agony splashed across your face with the jab of his knife. All you could wonder was what sick pleasure he took in being anonymous while he hurt you."

Lucas walked to her and ran his finger down the scar on her chin. "He's responsible for this?" Her nod was short. "Tell me exactly what he said to you that night, Lilah."

"The other guy always did the talking, but The Mask, he came in hot with the knife, sliced me up and left me for the other two guys to acquire—"

"Who always failed to?"

"Oddly enough, yes," she said with a shrug. "I could always escape their grip and run, but I knew they'd be back."

"Could that have been on purpose?"

"Like, they let me go?" she asked, and he nodded, adding a half a head tilt to make it questionable. Another shudder went through her before she answered. "You think they were just playing with me?"

"I don't know what to think other than he had a chance to slit your throat that night and didn't," he said, pointing at her chin and neck. "Instead, he stopped just short of slicing your carotid. He could have ended you being a problem six years ago instead of 'hunting' you for all of them," he said, adding air quotes. "It doesn't make sense." The more he studied the map and the list of attacks, the less sense it made. "What happened in year three when he showed up?"

If she thought he missed the subtle way she crossed her arms over her belly, she was wrong. "Same type of situation. He came in, tortured me a little and left me for the other two." She held up her hand. "Except he whispered that time."

"What did he say?"

Her tender throat bobbed once as her eyes went closed. "That the next time would be our last visit together. As the pawn, I can only move forward, not backward or sideways, the way he could as the king. He said I was surrounded and he'd made sure I had nowhere to go but where he sent me. He also said no one could help me now and that he'd be back to collect his pawn when he needed her to win the game."

An expletive fell from Lucas's lips before he walked to her and wrapped her in his arms. "I'm so sorry, darling. He's playing a game that only he understands. He didn't attack you with a knife the last two times?"

"Oh, yes," she whispered, a shiver spiking through her until he rubbed it away with his warm hand against her back. "He definitely attacked with a knife. He took extreme pleasure in hurting me."

Lucas stepped back and eyed her. "Where?"

"It doesn't matter, Luca," she said, but he caught the spike of fear in her eyes. "What matters is now I can't stop thinking that those guys let me go each time at The Mask's orders."

"Where, Lilah?" he asked again as though he hadn't heard her last sentence. "Tell me where."

He waited and watched the war reflected in her eyes

until she shook her head. "I'm not showing you." Her swallow was so harsh it was audible, and he stepped toward her again. "I will say that when he found me ten months ago, it was so bad I shouldn't have been able to fight them off or escape, but I did. Why didn't I think of that? They never wanted to capture me. They wanted to toy with me."

"Why do you think that is?"

She walked to the wall and stood in front of it. "They wanted to keep me off balance? They wanted me to move?"

"They wanted you too scared to go to the authorities?" Lucas asked, coming up behind her.

"Or to think the police wouldn't help me if I did go to them," she agreed. "Not that I ever did or could. With my clearance level, walking into a police station was a sure way to put Delilah Hartman back on the map."

"I hadn't thought of that, but you're right," he agreed. "Then they'd ask why you were using a different name. When he attacked you ten months ago, the words he whispered were chilling. He would come and collect his pawn, 'when he needed her to win the game.' Is that what made you believe this had something to do with the flash drive of information?"

"I didn't know what else it could be about, Lucas. I was afraid they knew I had read The Lost Key of Honor file and had information I shouldn't have."

"If that were the case, killing you would have been the right answer. The fact that they didn't makes me think you know something—"

"Or they think I know something," she interrupted. "Something I don't know."

"That you think you don't know, but you don't know what it is, so there's no way to know if you know it or not."

Lilah burst out laughing, nearly doubling over as her shoulders shook. When she got herself under control, even he was grinning despite the grim circumstances. "That was the most convoluted but understandable sentence I've ever heard. Whether I know something or not is beside the point because they think I do. What are we going to do with this mess?" she asked, letting her hand flick at the wall until it fell to her side.

"We're going to contact Mina and see if she can find out where Major Burris was on the dates The Mask attacked you."

Rather than respond, she just stood in one place and stared at him open-mouthed. "Are you—have you lost it? Major Burris?"

Lucas took her shoulders and forced eye contact with her. "We know your medal was most likely what they used to track you. That indicates military involvement. We also know the guys who are tracking you are ex-military. We know that all those artifacts that are missing shouldn't be. It's not a stretch to think Burris is somehow involved in this."

"It wasn't him," she said, shaking her head. "I know it wasn't him behind that mask. I didn't recognize his voice."

"Maybe not, but it doesn't hurt to have Mina find out where he was, right?"

"It's not him, Lucas."

"Humor me?"

Lilah motioned at the phone on the table and sat on

the bed to watch him type. He kept his facial expression neutral despite the fire raging through his veins. He wanted to find the man tormenting her and give him a taste of his own medicine. Right or wrong. He would do anything to protect Lilah now that she was back in his life, but he couldn't protect her from the pain and fear she suffered in the past, and that filled him with rage. He snapped the phone down on the desk and stalked toward her. "Show me."

"Show you what?" she asked, her head cocked to the side in confusion.

"Where The Mask cut you."

"Absolutely not," she said between clenched teeth.

"What are you afraid of, Lilah?"

"I'm not afraid of anything, Luca. What happened in the past should stay in the past."

"If I had a million dollars, I would bet all of it that where he cut you is why you turned me down on the once-and-done request yesterday."

"Wow," she said, drawing out the last *w*. "You do think highly of yourself."

"Not at all," he said, taking another step closer. "But I know you—"

"No, you knew me. There's a difference, Luca. I'm not the same woman who left that hospital. That woman is gone."

"Maybe some of her is gone, but the woman I held on my lap with my lips on hers in an old motel was the same woman I held on my lap with my lips on hers on a beach in the middle of Lake Superior. At least until that woman remembered she had something to hide."

The phone beeped, and she let out a relieved breath. "You better get that. It's Mina."

"She's on it," he said, dropping the phone to the desk. "Said she'd get back to us, as she had just gotten into the files on Burris's trial."

"Good. Maybe we'll finally get the information to move forward and clear my name." She turned and walked to Haven, patting him on the top of his head where he slept. When she turned back around, Lucas grasped her arm.

"You can pretend the past doesn't matter if that makes you feel better, but one day, I will find out what that animal did to you and I will kiss every last scar."

He dropped his voice to the timbre he knew always made her melt inside. The timbre that said he meant every word and what he said could be trusted.

"Just in case the destruction of my face isn't enough for you," she said, righteous indignation filling her words, "let me make it incredibly clear that I'm your past, Lucas, and you should be glad I am!"

With her fingers shaking and tears in her eyes, she lifted her shirt to reveal what she'd been hiding all this time. Unable to process the scene before him, he stumbled backward onto the bed without a word.

Chapter Seventeen

Pain flooded Delilah as the look on his face transformed from caring to stunned to horrified. She hated that she had to destroy the memory of what she used to be to him, but it didn't matter. When this was over, they'd part ways and this moment of humiliation could be stored in the box where she kept all of her Lucas Porter memories.

She turned away and walked to the window, pulling back the curtain to see the snow still falling and the sky getting darker. The sun set early as Christmas approached, and she couldn't help but wonder if she'd live to see her thirty-fourth Christmas. It used to be her favorite season—not for the decorations, goodies or gifts, but for the sense of hope and renewal it ushered in. When she was a child, her father was the one who made Christmas merry. He loved everything about the season, from the carols to the candy to the tree and treats. After he died, her mom worked hard to keep joy in the holiday, but there was always something missing.

Then she joined the service and spent her first Christmas away from home. She had struggled to find joy that first year, so she was surprised it came so easily to her in the midst of war. Delilah had found joy in singing

Christmas carols around a tiny tree and sharing treats sent by caring family members simply by reminding herself that Christmas, no matter the place, was a time for family. The soldiers on the base were her family, and she took comfort in having them. During war, Christmas was a time of hope for peace, even if that hope was always short-lived. That hadn't changed since she left the service. The last six Christmases she had spent alone but always took a moment to find joy in the day, and hope that it would be her last Christmas under wraps. It was then she realized, one way or the other, this was the end.

Her heart pulsed hard, and she rubbed her chest, but it didn't relieve the pain. Luca was everything she had wanted in her past life, but now he could be nothing to her, even if she wished their lives could be different. This would be their first and last Christmas together, leaving her with nothing but memories for every Christmas season to come—if she made it out of this alive, that is.

"My God," he whispered, his breath whooshing out again. "How did you survive something like that, Lilah?"

"He made sure to slice me just deep enough that I was maimed but not deep enough to kill me. It took forty-four stitches the first time and seventy-seven the second time to put me back together. The hospitals forced me to file a police report, but it didn't matter. The woman who walked into that hospital ceased to exist the moment she left."

"This sick animal needs to be stopped," Lucas said between clenched teeth. "We've got you now," he said, walking to where she stood at the window. "I know you don't need protecting, but I'm going to be here to fight with you until we find him and end this game he's playing."

"I want to believe that, but we've been together for two days and are no further ahead than when you found me."

"You're wrong. We have pieces of the puzzle, but we're missing the one pivotal piece that will bring the picture into focus and reveal the artist behind the design. You've fought too long and worked too hard to give up now."

Delilah knew that to be the truth. "But I only did it for you, Luca. I wanted to protect you."

"Then let me protect you now, my darling Delilah."

His words were desperate, and she turned just as he pulled her into him and took her lips, reminding her of all the reasons she had to keep those memories of Lucas locked up in a box. Allowing herself to feel them was too painful. Her heart and body couldn't take more pain. Still, she kissed him back, unable to deny herself the feel of his lips and the way his hot tongue cuddled hers.

"Lucas, we can't," she said, her lips still pressed to his. "We can't do this. It's not fair to either of us."

"Do you know what's not fair?" he asked, walking her backward to the bed. "Thinking I desire you less than I did before because of superficial scars on your skin. It's unfair to yourself and me. It's as though you think I'm superficial and never really cared about you."

"I don't think that, Luca," she whispered as he set her down on the edge of the bed and hoisted her up to the pillows. "When I say it's unfair, I mean it's unfair to ourselves knowing we can never be together again."

"Never is a dangerous word, Delilah Hartman. I never

thought I'd see you again, but here you are, under my lips, reminding me why you never left my mind all these years. Why you were the last thought I had every day and the first every morning."

He lifted her shirt while he whispered sweet nothings, letting the cool air brush across her tender skin. She had a decision to make. Stop this now and continue to fight against the current trying to pull them under, or let herself have a moment of pleasure in a world full of pain.

His lips feathered a kiss across where her naval used to be before the ropy scar took over in a morbid smiley face. With a sharp intake of breath, her belly quivered as he moved his lips to the left and kissed her again, following the trail of the scar to her rib cage. His hands, so familiar against her skin, wrapped around her torso and pushed the shirt to her bra, making room for his lips as he traced another jagged scar to the right and down to her hip.

How was she supposed to fight against this when it felt so good? So right? His words came back to her. Once and done. It would never be done for her, but as he trailed his tongue across another scar, she decided once was better than none.

"Luca," she whispered, her breath heavy in her chest. When he lifted his head, his pupils were dilated and filled with heady need. "We don't have any protection."

A wicked smile lifted his lips as he rose and rifled through a bag beside the bed. He came up with a silver package in his hand. "Secure One has us covered," he promised, tossing it on the nightstand before he went back to kissing her belly, drawing a moan from her lips.

The sound was fuel to his flame, and he tossed her

glasses on the nightstand, stripped her of her shirt and, just as quickly, her bra. He leaned back on his knees, his gaze raking her breasts. "You're even more beautiful than the last time I made love to you. I didn't think that was possible. Softer. Sweeter," he whispered, his head dipping to tease a nipple with his tongue.

"The last six years haven't been kind to my body," she whispered, her hands sliding into his soft locks.

He lifted his head and took her lips for a hot ride through the past. "Darling, your body is my resting place. Always has been. That hasn't changed."

Rather than answer, she slid her hands under his shirt until he grasped the hem and pulled it over his head, letting it sail across the room. Her hands roamed over his muscles while he quickly did away with their boots and cargo pants. He loomed over her, his gaze filled with flames, and then, slowly and with the utmost tenderness, he lowered himself to rest gently across her body, their lips perfectly aligned.

He closed his eyes as his lips neared hers. "I have dreamed about this day for so long, Lilah. To cover you again and let your aura raise my soul from its resting place. To forget about everything for the moments that we're joined as one."

His honesty brought tears to her eyes, and she reached up to stroke his cheek before she grasped the package from the nightstand and tore it open. "Let's be one then and forget about anything but how we make each other feel."

Lucas dove in for a kiss while she deftly rolled the sheath over him, drawing a moan from deep in his throat. The room quieted for a single breath as he filled her before he swallowed her soft moan with his lips. Fire built in her belly, spiraling until her legs shook and her nails raked his back while she begged him to let her go. To let her fly into the sky and for him to be there with her, holding her hand as they soared.

"Patience, beautiful," he whispered, thrusting forward again as he nipped her earlobe. "We only get one second chance, and I'm going to cherish every last second of it."

With her head pressed into the pillow, she raised her hips, allowing him to slip a bit deeper to nestle in the place he loved the most. He told her that spot, that little piece of heaven, was his dwelling place.

"Lilah!" he exclaimed, his hips pressed tightly to hers. "I'm home." He whispered those two words into her ear as he thrust one more time and carried her over the threshold and into a second chance at life together.

"SECURE ONE, WHISKEY."

Lucas quickly moved to the desk and connected the computer. "Secure two, Lima." His gaze darted to Lilah, who was asleep on the bed. After they'd made love twice, she had showered and fallen into an exhausted slumber. He didn't want to wake her, so he addressed Mina quickly with a finger to his lips.

"She's exhausted," he said, without adding the part about how he was responsible for it.

"I can understand why. This is a nightmare of a dumpster fire, and none of us have an extinguisher."

Lucas couldn't help but chuckle. Leave it to Mina to sum it up so perfectly. "I couldn't agree more."

"I can't even imagine dealing with this alone the way

she has been for so many years. It's one twisted mess. I'm not sure we'll ever get to the bottom of it, but I'm not giving up. That said, dealing with the government is like entering the second level of hell whenever you need information."

"You're not wrong," he agreed, his gaze sliding to the bed again to check on Lilah. "Did you find anything?"

"I found some interesting tidbits, but still no trunk. It's like it never existed in the world, even though we know it did."

"Lilah searched a bunch of archives, too, but never found proof that it was in the possession of a history museum in the United States. There was also no history of it being returned to its rightful country."

"What's going on?" Lilah asked behind him, rubbing her face several times before climbing out from under the blanket he'd covered her with when she fell asleep. Thankfully, she had been fully dressed.

Lucas's cheeks heated, and his body stirred at the thought of holding her again, but he had to accept that their second chance had come and gone. Once she was free, the last place she'd want to be was confined within the walls of Secure One. Unfortunately for him, he needed those confines to feel safe. For a brief moment, while buried deep inside her, he wondered if he could be safe wherever she was, but he knew the truth. He was far more likely to hurt her when his world wasn't stable, and that was the last thing he wanted. She was happy with one and done, so he had no choice but to accept the same—even if it had been two and never done for him.

"I was just telling Lucas what a dumpster fire this mess is."

Lilah's laughter filled the room as she walked toward him until he could feel her heat wrap him up tightly again. "I wish I could say you're wrong, but I can't. It makes less and less sense the deeper we dig."

"Well, what I have to tell you also aligns with that."

"Oh, boy," Lucas said as he stood and offered Lilah the chair. "What did you find?"

"I'm glad you're sitting down," Mina said, her lips twisted into a grimaced smile. "When I got down to the paperwork regarding Burris's war crimes—" she put the words in quotations "—you're listed as a key witness to the events."

"I'm what now?" she asked, leaning in as though she hadn't heard her right. "I'm not sure I understand. The paperwork says I turned him in?"

"No, I can't see who turned him in. Just that you are listed as a key witness to the crimes."

"The crimes he didn't commit or go to jail for?"

Mina pointed at her with a nod. "Did you witness Major Burris commit any war crimes?"

"Seriously?" Lilah asked, her voice full of frustration and anger. "I worked with him only while I was in Germany. I was a computer geek. I had nothing to do with what was happening on the field."

"That's not true," Lucas said, leaning on the back of her chair with both hands to avoid touching her how he wanted to. Mina couldn't suspect there was more than friendship between them, or she'd insist that Cal replace him with someone who could be impartial about the situation. That wouldn't be necessary. As a soldier, he'd learned to separate his personal life from his professional, and he could do the same now, even if his personal life was at the heart of this professional situation. "You were tracking the ops and fielding any issues with the technology."

"Which," Mina said with a tip of her head, "if Burris was committing war crimes using the operations you were tracking, would make you a key witness."

"Even if I wasn't aware?"

"That is the question," Mina agreed. "You can be a witness to a crime without knowing, but that doesn't mean you can testify to those crimes in any way."

"The next question is, why wasn't I notified that I was considered a witness?" Lilah asked, her voice loud and clear now that the sleep and shock had disappeared. "And why wasn't I called to make a statement before they released him from the charges?"

"Those are also questions I can't answer other than..." She paused and shifted in her chair, obviously uncomfortable and not because of the pregnancy. She wasn't comfortable with what she had to say next.

"Other than?" Lilah asked. "Be straight with me, Mina. If this all comes down to something that happened in the service that I'm not aware of, I'd like to get it straightened out and get my life back before more years are stolen." Delilah tipped her head up to make eye contact with Lucas. He tried to keep his smile easy, when all he wanted to do was pull her into his arms and protect her from all of this.

"I wonder if the information I can see has been doctored."

"Whatever for?" Lilah asked. "Why would they need to doctor paperwork to make it look like I was a witness to something I wasn't a witness to?"

"As a reason to track you," Lucas said without hesitation.

Mina tipped her head in agreement. "That was my first thought, too."

"Tracking me is one thing. Attempted murder is something else entirely."

"I did warn you that this would make no sense," Mina said with a shrug. "As for Burris, he's living near Rochester now with his wife. He isn't working anywhere, but is heavily involved in several veteran organizations."

"Nothing else nefarious?" Lilah asked.

"On Burris? Not yet, but I will search property records, vehicles and bank situations. I came across something else that I thought was definitely concerning."

That got Lucas's attention, and he spun around a chair to straddle it. "How concerning?"

"Deadly," she said, her lips thinning for a moment. "It may be nothing, but I was hoping Delilah could shed some light on it."

"I'll do my best, but I've been out of touch with the world for years."

"While I was researching Burris," she said, shuffling papers around until she grabbed one from the pile, "I found the names of four other logistics officers listed as key witnesses to his war crimes."

"That's not surprising," Lilah said. "The supply chain in the military is massive. There were a lot of logistics officers."

"Agreed," Mina said, flicking her eyes to Lucas. The look she gave him said what came next was the surprising part. He put his arm around Lilah to ground her.

"When I searched those women, I discovered all four of them are dead."

The room was silent for two beats before Lilah spoke. "They're what now?"

"Dead," Mina repeated. "All victims of violent crimes."

"Did they involve knives?" Lilah asked, and Lucas heard her voice quiver on the last word.

"Three of the four," Mina answered. "This is the part that confuses me. All four of them were living under an alias like you. The first two women were found in an alley, as though it was a mugging gone wrong. Ultimately, their fingerprints were used to identify them since their identifications were poor fakes. Another woman was found naked in bed. It was staged to look like a BDSM scene gone wrong, but she had been strangled and moved to the bed. The final woman was pulled from a river. Whoever killed her made it look like she jumped, but the police have questions since she was obviously stabbed before she went into the river. That victim was also using a false name."

"I have questions," Lucas said, rubbing Lilah's back to keep her grounded. A shudder went through her, and he gently squeezed her neck to comfort her. As her anxiety built, Haven raised his head, assessed the situation and walked to Lilah, resting his head on her leg. Lucas noticed her stroke his head, and her shoulders relaxed as she did.

"The deaths of four women who did the same job I did is not a coincidence, Mina."

"You won't get an argument out of me. It is a dead end since the crimes were never solved. They remain open, but the last death was a year ago, so they're all cold cases now."

"Wait," Lucas said, leaning forward. "When did they find the first woman?"

Mina searched the paper and counted backward. "Almost five years ago. The next woman was found three years ago, the third was two years ago, and the river victim was last year."

"I was next," Lilah said, her voice surprisingly steady. "That's why The Mask showed up at the apartment building this time. It was my turn to die."

"The Mask?" Mina asked, glancing between them.

"That's what she called him," Lucas said before Lilah could. He didn't want her to have to explain it. "He did that to her chin and cut her several other places."

"I noticed the scars when you were dressing," Mina admitted, addressing Lilah now. "I'm so sorry that happened to you."

"Lucas pointed out that any of the three times he attacked me, he could have killed me." Mina nodded her agreement. "It was about ten months ago when he showed up and whispered in my ear. He said I was his pawn and he'd come for me when it was time for him to win the game."

"That's what finally spurred her to contact me," Lucas explained. "When he showed up a few weeks ago, she knew she was out of time."

"I was hoping to use the flash drive as a bargaining chip for my life," Lilah said, sarcastic laughter filling the room. "That was never going to happen."

"I'm curious as to why these other women were killed,

though," Mina said, flipping the camera to show the entire room since Cal and Eric had walked in.

"Is it possible you weren't the only one shipping artifacts back to the States?" Cal asked, sitting down at the table.

"I never considered it, but there had to be people on other bases also taking in antiquities to protect, right? There were other bases in other parts of those countries. You would think word would spread like wildfire throughout the curator community that we would keep their treasures safe. Do you have the real names of the women who were killed, Mina?"

Mina nodded and read off the women's names and ranks, but Delilah shook her head before she finished.

"I don't know any of them. Not that unusual, as I was working more cybersecurity than supply chain by that point in the war, but what is unusual is that they all died questionable deaths."

"And the timeline is scarily precise," Mina finished. "As though someone was checking off a box once something was completed."

"We just need to know what that something was and who was killing them," Lilah said with a groan. "Were there any other witnesses listed on the paperwork?"

"No, it was the five of you, and you're the only one left standing."

Lucas tipped his head to the side. "Mina, did any of those women get medals for their service?"

"Boy, I didn't dig that far. Do you think it's important?"

"I do," Cal said. "That's why we're here. Eric retrieved the medal from the abandoned house today."

"It was still there?" Lilah asked. "I figured if they were tracking me with it, they'd take it."

"They might have if they had time to search for it," Eric said, pulling out a chair. "But the medal was in the tree with the camera. I put it there to protect it. It would lead them to the house, but my gut said the tracker wasn't pinpoint accurate."

"Meaning it just gave them a general area she was in?" Lucas asked.

"Exactly," Eric agreed as he pulled it from his pocket. The medal was in two parts now as he laid them on the table. "I apologize that it's ruined," he said to Lilah, who shrugged as though she no longer cared. "When I broke it open, inside was the smallest GPS I've ever seen. Lucas, you were right. It was solar powered."

"You didn't bring it back to base with you, right?" Lucas asked, and Eric shook his head.

"No, that's why I did it in the field. I left the tracker in the tree. If they tag it again, it will get plenty of power to keep it active. I wasn't sure if we'd need it for evidence, so I didn't want to destroy it."

"All of that said, what's our next move?" Lucas asked.

The room fell silent until Lilah spoke. "I think it's time we pay my old major a little visit."

"No. Not happening," Lucas said, leaning over the chair and grasping her shoulders. "You're not going any-where near him."

"Do you have a better idea?" Delilah asked, her gaze locked with his as though the rest of the team no longer existed in the conversation. "You know what they say. If you want the truth, get it straight from the horse's mouth."

"She's not wrong," Mina said from the computer.

"You're not helping, Mina," Lucas snapped.

"She is, though," Lilah reminded him. "That's why this has to end. I've gotten so many people involved in this nightmare, including you. It's my responsibility to get you back out of it alive and in one piece. I can't do that holed up in this motel room!"

"I don't like it," Lucas said, his hand fisted in his hair. "We don't have enough information to walk into a mission we don't understand and expect to come out unscathed."

"I don't like it, either," Mina and Cal said in unison, giving the moment a bit of levity. "But she's right," Mina finished. "There is no way to solve this from that motel room. Let us talk together as a team about options. We'll call you back?"

Lucas shook his head in defeat. "Fine, but I already know this is not smart."

"Maybe, but I'm not sure we have any other move on the board. Whiskey, out."

The screen went black, and the room went silent.

"Luca," Lilah finally said, her voice soft in the quiet of the room. "You know I'm right about this."

The answer he had to give was one she wouldn't like, so he said nothing while he shrugged on his field coat and grabbed Haven's lead. "We're going to check the perimeter. Lock the door behind me."

"Luca," she called as he opened the door and walked out into the blackness, but he let the night swallow anything else she had to say.

Chapter Eighteen

If Lucas was going to agree to this plan, Delilah needed to find a tidbit of information to prove that going to Burris was the only answer, even if she already knew it was the only answer. She didn't know how she knew, but something told her the only way to find the end was to start at the beginning.

That was her plan as she opened The Lost Key of Honor file again and started scrolling. She had read it so many times that nothing stuck out to her as applicable. There had to be something, though. Claiming five women were witnesses to something they couldn't back up with facts just to kill them didn't make sense otherwise. Then again, if Lucas was right, and the war crimes occurred during the ops, she'd be in charge of troubleshooting, so it was possible she had information and didn't know it. That honestly felt like the only answer as she scrolled down the rows, because the file revealed nothing it hadn't already. All this correspondence was nothing more than a back-and-forth sharing of buildings checked, people contacted and the next steps.

While she read, her mind wandered back to the time spent in bed with Lucas. They'd gone as slow as they could the first time they'd made love, but it was still too fast. The second time had been more about learning how they had changed and discovering how they had stayed the same. Their touch had been gentler, longer and more precise, leading to an intimacy they hadn't shared that first summer. She knew why, too. That summer, they thought they'd be together forever. This Christmas, they knew their time together was fleeting.

Someone in the room next door dropped something, and Delilah jumped, accidentally clicking the mouse on the file. That click brought up a box asking her if she wanted to go to the link provided. Did she? Yes. Could she? Her gaze tracked to the VPN that had her as a user based in Switzerland. There were ways to see a VPN, but she hoped the file no longer mattered or they would take it at face value if they noticed anyone on the link. Her laughter filled the room. No, they'd know immediately that Delilah Hartman had clicked the link, but Cal's stealth VPN was impossible to get around. It offered her a cloak of invisibility she never had before when online. If ever there was a time to take advantage of it, now was that time.

A click on the yes button took her to a chat website and into a private room. There was a chat transcript going back eight years, with the latest entries from someone named *Iamthatguy* being one month ago when he'd replied to someone called *Bigmanoncampus*.

Any luck this time?

None. I don't believe this tablet exists anymore. If it did, it surely would have been found by now.

I don't care what you believe. The tablet is out there.

Do you have any new leads? I sure as hell don't. It may be time to let it go, boss.

Don't tell me to let it go! We're a month from the big event and we still don't have the main attraction! I've got a new lead, but I'll need you to go back to where this started. The information will come in the usual manner. I'll be waiting to hear.

When *Iamthatguy* responded, he certainly didn't sound happy.

Back to the beginning? This is exhausting and I'm not getting any younger. I'll go one last time, but after that, I'm out.

You're out when I say you're out! *Bigmanoncampus* replied. Delilah could almost hear the venom dripping from his words. Get the job done, we're running out of time! If you don't, you'll be spending your Christmas in a very small box.

Delilah had no doubt they were talking about the tablet to open the trunk. Undeterred, she scrolled up to a feature where items could be pinned, curious about the files and why they would pin them there. She clicked open the first file and was surprised to see a map of a small village in Iraq. It had been methodically marked off with a red *x* through each building on the image. The following three files she opened were the same.

The fourth was a list of names with red lines drawn through each one.

"The snow has stopped, but with that fresh layer on the ground, it's cold," Lucas said, coming back inside with a snow-covered Haven. His return surprised her, and she glanced up to see him strip off his coat and pull off Haven's boots.

"How long have you been out there?"

"Too long," he answered, motioning for Haven to follow him to his food bowl. "But I cleared the van of snow so we can go."

"You agree that we need to find Burris?" she asked, her tone giving away her surprise.

"No, but we also can't stay here much longer." She could tell he was trying not to be short with her when all he wanted to do was shake her silly until she understood what a bad idea it was to show up on Burris's doorstep. She completely understood what a bad idea it was, but that didn't mean she had a choice. Lucas would end up on the run with her if they didn't do something soon. While she wouldn't mind that, something told her Cal and the other guys at Secure One would. No, it was time, once and for all, to find out what they wanted from her and give it to them. If they wanted her, she'd turn herself over to the US government and hope for the best. She couldn't continue to put other people at risk because she was afraid.

Her spine stiffened with the thought, and she turned back to the computer. There was one more file, and she clicked it open, but this time, page after page after page opened. "What is going on?" she muttered as Lucas came up behind her.

"What are you looking at?"

Without turning, she quickly flipped through the pages, stopping long enough to glance through each one. "I accidentally clicked inside the file for The Lost Key of Honor. It took me to this chat room–type website where *Iamthatguy* and *Bigmanoncampus* discuss their search for the missing tablet. This," she said, motioning at the screen, "has maps of villages in Iraq that were searched, and these," she tapped the open file on her screen, "are detailed dossiers on what I think are other artifacts they found during the search." She took a moment to read more of each file, a whistle escaping as she recognized several artifacts on the list she had been told to catalog. "What in the world?" The question was barely whispered as her hand froze on the mouse.

"What did you find?" he asked, kneeling beside her chair.

Her finger shaking, she pointed at the screen. "The trunk hasn't disappeared. Whoever these two guys are have it in their possession."

"They want access to it so when they find the tablet, they can open the trunk."

"Feels a little Indiana Jones in here, right?" Delilah asked, leaning back in the chair. "We all know that never ended well for the greedy treasure hunters."

Lucas stood and started to massage her shoulders again, almost like he knew she needed a calming hand at the helm. "It's not going to work out for these guys, either, once we find out who they are, that is. Is there a way to send these to Mina?"

"I can't download them," she said, checking the files' properties. "I could just send her the whole file." She

bit her lip and stared at the screen. If she shared The
Lost Key of Honor file with Mina, that made her a witness to anything illegal they found in the files and an
accomplice to data theft. She didn't want to put that on
Mina's or Secure One's back. Then again, considering
what Mina did there, it wouldn't be her first rodeo with
backdoor access to files.

"What are you thinking? Walk me through it," he en-
couraged, still massaging her shoulders.

"I could send Mina a digital copy of the entire flash
drive. Then she'd have The Lost Key of Honor file and
access to all of this and the full dossier on each artifact.
The problem is that makes her a witness to any crimes
we discover and an accomplice to any data we use to
bring this to an end."

"Darling, if Mina was worried about being an accomplice to data theft, she wouldn't be doing what she's
doing. Send her the file."

"Somehow, I knew you were going to say that."
Laughter spilled from her lips, and it felt good amid all
the angst that filled her.

Delilah enlarged the first open file and opened the
snipping tool app.

"What are you doing? I thought you said you can't
save the files."

"I can't, not in the traditional way, but I can take screenshots. There's a fifty-fifty chance that the chat room ceases
to exist as soon as I close this tab."

"What now?" he asked, leaning on the desk, ankles
crossed. "Why would it cease to exist?"

"There could be a failsafe on it, so if anyone but them
login, it shuts itself down."

"Wouldn't that happen right away? It's letting you read it."

Delilah kept at her task as she talked, afraid he was right and the screen could go black any second. "I followed the link from the file, making the page think I was one of them, but I'm not taking any chances that Mina can't get back in to read this stuff." After a few more clicks of the mouse, she saved everything in a new file. While at it, she saved the chat in a sequence of screenshots and then highlighted the dates for Mina to see. "Okay, I think I have it all." She clicked out of the chat room and let out a sigh.

"Package that up and send it to Mina. Then, we're leaving."

"To go where?" she asked, adding the files to the flash drive and zipping the contents.

He held up his phone. "We're about to find out. Is that ready to go to her?" Delilah nodded, and Lucas hit the call button, holding the screen out for her to see. "Secure one, Lima," Luca said, waiting for a beat until they heard Mina's reply. When her face filled the screen, it was lined with fatigue. Delilah immediately felt guilty for putting this on their shoulders. What made her feel a little better was knowing this was almost over. They could all go back to their lives, even if she was lost to time forever.

THE VAN WAS unnaturally quiet. It was as though they were holding their breath, knowing something big was coming but unsure if they'd survive whatever it was. When the team called back, they sent them south, sticking to back roads and two-lane highways to avoid the freeway. Mina programmed the van's GPS with the location of Burris's house in Rochester. They'd head in that direction while she went through the files on the flash drive Lilah had sent.

He glanced at the woman in the seat next to him and fought back the wave of protectiveness that filled him. Hard as it was, he couldn't protect her from this. The only way out of it was through it. He feared the through part would leave them both shredded and bleeding. Four women were already dead. There was no way he would let her be the next one. What he was struggling to understand was, while a pet project wasn't unusual for the military, hiding other countries' treasures was immoral at best and illegal at worst. The US government would never sanction that. The only thing worse would be auctioning them off to the highest bidder. Lucas gasped.

Lilah glanced at him immediately. "What?" she asked. "Are you okay?"

"Fine, but I was just thinking. Do you think the two guys from the chat room plan to sell the artifacts on the black market?"

"Well, yeah. Going by the dates in the chat room, my bet is, they have an auction scheduled on Christmas Day. They want the tablet to complete the trunk, thereby making it the main attraction. It will surely bring a bidding war unlike any ever seen."

"Christmas Day?"

"He said the big event was in a month, counting forward that makes it Christmas Day. I see the allure of the ultrarich wanting a new trinket on that day."

"Okay, but how do you find buyers for stolen artifacts? It's not like you can use Sotheby's."

He couldn't help but smile when she laughed. He loved being the one to make her laugh now that they were together again. At least for however long they were together. This second chance of theirs could end quickly and without warning. That thought stole the smile from his lips.

"The black market is deep and dark, Luca. There are plenty of buyers for these artifacts who are all too happy to keep them locked away from the world forever. We can't let that happen."

"This *Bigmanoncampus* and *Iamthatguy*, do you think they're military?"

"I did get to the page via the file, so that would make the most sense."

"True." Lucas drove in silence for a few moments. "But what if the military is monitoring the page for intel?"

"Could be that, too," she agreed. "There's no way to know unless we can see who's behind the fake names, which I doubt even Mina can do. Not on the dark web like that."

"Wait, that was the dark web?"

"Uh, yeah," she said, biting her lip. "I thought you knew."

"I'm not a computer nerd, Lilah. I thought it was just a web page."

"Who you calling a computer nerd?" she asked haughtily before they both giggled.

It was several miles down the road before they got themselves together again. "Okay, this is serious business," Lucas said, but his smile defied that statement. He loved being with her again and refused to think about how boring life would be when she was gone.

"We already know these artifacts aren't in the museums," Lilah said, leaning back into the seat. "Which means they have to be somewhere else. They may not even be in the country at this point."

"I wish we knew if that chat room was being monitored by the military, created by them or owned by someone else entirely."

Lilah nodded, ready to speak, when the phone rang, making them both jump. Lucas hit the answer button on the dashboard. "Secure one, Lima."

"Secure two, Whiskey," Mina said.

"Did you find something?" Lilah asked, sitting forward in her seat to turn up the volume. Lucas scanned the road for somewhere to pull over and noticed an old rest stop ahead.

"Hang on, Mina, I'm going to pull over." He slowed, turned and pulled the van under overgrown trees before he doused the headlights. There was no sense in being a sitting target if someone was looking for them. "Go ahead."

"I haven't had time to go through all of the flash drive files yet, but I did get results for the property search on Burris."

Lilah glanced at Lucas quizzically. "I thought we knew that already. Isn't that why we're driving to Rochester?"

"Yes, he has a home in Rochester, but he also has hunting land southwest of the Rochester airport."

"There's hunting land all over that part of Minnesota. I'm not sure how that helps us," Lucas said, frustrated by the lack of answers at every turn.

"It may be nothing, but he applied for a building permit to put up a garage on that land. Said he was going to store his hunting equipment in it."

"That makes sense," Lucas said, a huff leaving his lips as he let out a long, frustrated breath. "We're in hunting country. You know that, Mina."

"I do," she agreed, "which is why I checked DNR records next. George Burris has never had a hunting license in his life."

Chapter Nineteen

Lilah's heart pounded hard at Mina's revelation. "You think he built the garage for other purposes?"

"I see no other reason than to store something," Mina agreed. "It could be innocent, but I'm starting to think it's not."

"Me, too," Luca agreed.

"Especially since we can't find evidence that any of those artifacts in your files ever made it to a museum."

"What is the working theory then, Mina?" Lucas asked, rubbing his hands on his thighs before he tapped out a rhythm in threes. He felt exposed sitting in such an isolated location and wanted to get out of there. Haven stuck his snout around the side of the seat to bop his arm. It was a reminder to breathe, so he inhaled to three and held it, counting to three while he waited for Mina to answer.

"I think we all know the answer to that question," Mina said.

"That Burris has somehow managed to funnel all these artifacts to a garage in Minnesota?" Lilah asked.

"With or without help from someone else," Mina agreed. "The how—I can't answer that. The why, well, the simple answer is money."

"Did you get into the chat room?" Lilah asked out of curiosity.

"No, you were right about it locking me out. I clicked around on the file, but it went nowhere."

"Let me give you the highlights," Lilah said. "I think they're planning an auction for Christmas Day and wanted the trunk complete to encourage a bidding war."

"We can't let that happen," Mina vehemently said. "If that's the case, we have three days to stop it."

"Are they onto us?" Luca asked, his gaze tracking the area around the van with caution.

"No, they're onto the fact that someone else was in the chat room. I assume they were notified. The dark web is tricky, as Lilah knows."

"That's why I took the screenshots," she said. "I was relatively sure that's what was going to happen."

"You told me it was a fifty-fifty chance," Luca said, turning to face her.

"I didn't want to freak you out," Lilah admitted to Mina's laughter.

"We still have no proof that Burris is behind this, though," Lilah said. "It's just a gut feeling on our part."

"I always go with the gut," Mina said. "It's rarely wrong."

"I'm feeling exposed out here without backup," Lucas said. "I don't want to approach this place alone."

"That's why the main team is getting ready to leave. They'll meet you at the Rochester airport at 0800 hours."

"We'll be in Rochester in an hour," Luca said, eyeing the clock that read 5:00 a.m.

"Head to the airport and wait for the rest of the team. Since the chat room won't let me in, I can't dig into who the two people are conversing on it. I'd bet my firstborn that one of them is Burris."

Luca's laughter filled the van. "Roman wouldn't be happy with you betting his little girl, but I agree."

"Me, too," Lilah said, a lead weight settling into her gut. "That would explain the tracker in the medal. If he'd been led to believe I was a witness, he'd be nervous since we worked so closely together on what I thought was preserving these artifacts. Instead, he was looting them to sell illegally and killing anyone who knew about it. I guess, in a way, that does make me culpable."

"No," Luca and Mina said together. "You were following orders," Mina said. "You had no way to know that the artifacts weren't going where you sent them. Someone was cutting them off at the pass. I aim to find that person, but so many years have passed that it may be impossible."

"I need to get back on the road," Lucas said, his nerves frayed. "We'll meet the team at 0800 hours unless we hear otherwise. If you need anything, you know how to reach us."

"Ten-four. Whiskey out."

Luca glanced at her. "With any luck, we'll find something useful at the property."

"And then what?" Lilah asked. "If we find proof of something, and I report it, they're going to accuse me of the crime since I have no proof that I didn't know the artifacts weren't being shipped properly."

"You've been on the run for six years!" Luca ground out. "Why else would you run?"

"On the run can mean a lot of things. They could say I was running from the law, not for my life."

"I think the scars covering your body would say otherwise, Lilah."

She sat nodding, trying to figure out what was bothering her. "Burris isn't The Mask, though. I know for sure he's not the guy coming after me."

"That doesn't mean he isn't involved," Luca responded, flipping on the headlights and putting the van back into Drive. "The Mask could be another hired thug."

"True, but it felt far too personal for any old thug. It's like the man behind the mask has a personal vendetta against me."

"Like he couldn't kill you yet, but he needed to keep you off-kilter and afraid."

"That," she said without thought. "It makes me wonder if that's why he came at me at regular intervals. He never wanted me to get comfortable with the idea that he was gone for good or that I wasn't being watched. Regardless, I could still get trapped in this, Luca. I could go to prison for all of this."

"That's where you're wrong. The information on that flash drive proves that you didn't know what was happening. It shows a straight chain of command. The items went to central shipping when they left your hands. Your major signed off on that. There was no way for you to know they didn't get to their next destination. Your responsibility ended when Burris signed off."

"When Burris signed off," she said slowly. "Burris had to sign off, which means he could have easily changed or deleted all of my shipping labels. He could have shipped them elsewhere or moved them out of the countries in other ways. That might be our proof that Burris is behind this. Regardless, I'm scared this will blow up in my face and I'll be left holding the bag. Worse yet, it blows back on you and Secure One."

"Let's take this one step at a time, okay?" he asked, reaching out to take her hand and squeeze it.

"What happens if we don't find anything at Burris's property?"

"I guess we wait for Mina to find us another lead."

"No," she said, her head shaking as she thought about the future. "I'm done running. If we don't find anything at the property, I'll confront Burris—alone."

"You are absolutely not doing that," Lucas said between clenched teeth. "Selina tried that and nearly died at the hands of the person after her. On the off chance Burris is The Mask, I refuse to let you take that risk. Backed into a corner, he might stop cutting and start killing."

Lilah bit her tongue to keep from arguing with him. He was wrong, but he was also right. She was stuck between a rock and a hard place that might only be solved by her sticking her neck out. Luca may not understand that, but as the final puzzle piece snapped into place, she did. Burris wasn't The Mask. With a sinking heart, she realized who it was.

"CAL IS NOT going to be happy about this," Lucas whispered for the third time, but Lilah wasn't listening. "We were supposed to wait for them."

"We are waiting," she answered. "He didn't say we couldn't approach Burris's other property."

"I'm rather sure he meant in general, Lilah," he said between clenched teeth. He'd been trying to get her to listen to him for the last hour, but she wasn't budging. She was keeping something from him, and he didn't know what it was, but ever since they left that rest stop, she'd been withdrawn and somber.

"Hold up a minute," he said, pulling her and Haven into a grove of trees near Burris's property line. The houses were spaced far apart, with at least an acre of land surrounded by woods that made for natural fencing. They would have to do it methodically if they approached the Burris home. The last thing he wanted was for someone to call the cops. "What is going on with you? Since Mina called about Burris's other property, you've been uncommunicative, combative and bossy."

She stood before him with stubbornness written across her features in a way that said she wanted to tell him the truth but was determined not to in order to protect him. Lucas wasn't having it. He wrapped his arms around her and pulled him into her, kissing her forehead before he leaned down near her ear. "I'm already involved in this, Lilah. I'm already involved with you. We can't deny that, but I can protect you. Just tell me what you're thinking. Have you even thought this through?" He paused and put his lips on hers, but sensing her hesitation and fear, he pulled back. "You haven't, but you know it needs to end, so you're willing to sacrifice yourself to protect me."

"You're right, I am!" she exclaimed, tapping him in the chest. "I need to stop dragging other people into this nightmare and stand ready to defend myself and my country. That's the oath I took in the army and the one I hold myself to today. You don't have to like that choice, but you do have to respect it." A tear tracked down her cheek, and he pulled off her glasses, wiping the tears with his thumb. "No more innocents can lose their lives because of me, Luca. Enough people have already died due to greed and corruption. It's on me to stop this now. I understand if you want no part of it. Take Haven, get in the van and go home. You can't save me now. I'll pay the piper, whatever the cost, so no one else has to. That's the only right and fair thing to do."

A tendril of anger worked its way from his gut into his throat. Anger for the men who started this mess and at her for thinking she had to go this alone. "For the longest time, I was mad at you, Delilah Hartman, but never as mad as I am now. I'm standing alongside you, ready to defend you or go down trying, but you want to play the hero and do it all yourself!"

"That's not what I'm doing! I'm giving you a damn out before things get real, Luca. This isn't your war to fight. It's mine. I won't ask you to walk back into battle for me again."

He grasped her face in his hands and brought her lips to his, drinking from her like a man who hadn't had water in days. When the kiss ended, he held her gaze, the sky lightening enough for him to see the look in her eyes that said he had to go all in if he wanted her to listen. "You're not asking me. I'm volunteering. I would walk into any battle with you, Delilah Hartman. I'd rather die by your side than live without you again. Do you understand what I'm saying?" Her nod was enough for him. "You haven't been able to trust anyone for a long time, and I understand that, but you could always trust me, right?"

"Always," she said, her words breathy on the cold morning air.

"Then trust me this time, the most important time

of your life, Lilah. Let us help you end this war. No one fights alone. You have special ops cops and a sharpshooter headed here to fight with you. They wouldn't do that if they didn't think the fight was worth it. You can trust them for the simple reason that I trust them."

The silent morning stretched between them as smoky tendrils rose from the trees, warmed by the rising sun. Haven leaned into him, checking his handler for shakiness that wasn't there. Lucas was firm in his declaration to this woman, and he would wait however long it took for her to accept it and make the right decision.

"I'm terrified, Luca. Terrified that I'll die and terrified that you will. I don't know what the right answer is anymore."

He rubbed his thumb across her forehead and smiled. "I know you don't. That's understandable. You want this to be over, but you see no other way than to walk in guns blazing. Trust me when I say Secure One has your back."

When her shoulders deflated a hair, Lucas knew she'd made her decision. His heart nearly broke in two when she nodded, biting her lip to keep it from trembling. "Let's go meet the rest of the team and make a better plan. I'm not in the mood to die today."

The truth spoken, he leaned in and kissed her, gently this time, pouring all of his soothing care into her. No one needed it more than her after all these years alone. When the kiss ended, she smiled at him, her gloved hand patting his face. "Thank you for being my voice of reason in a world where nothing makes sense."

"I'll continue to be until this is over," he promised as they returned to the van. He secured Haven while she climbed in, then joined her and started the van. He cranked the heat up to warm them after being out in the cold.

"Secure one, Charlie." Cal's voice filled the van, and Lucas hit the answer button on the dashboard.

"Secure two, Lima."

"Why in the hell is my van outside George Burris's home? I will not have another team member go rogue on me!"

"It's my fault, sir," Lilah said without hesitation. "I thought I had to fight this battle alone, but Luca convinced me otherwise. Don't be upset with him."

"I was never going to let her go in there, boss."

"I didn't think you would, son."

"You don't sound like you're in the air yet," Lilah said, her head tipped as she listened to the background noise.

"We're not. Plans changed. I decided filing a flight plan might tip someone off to your presence there. Besides, bringing mobile command is easier when we don't know what we're up against. Roman, what's our ETA?"

"We'll hit Rochester proper in an hour and thirty-seven minutes. I need you to scout a location for us to circle the wagons and then send us the coordinates."

"We're headed in the direction of the airport now. You'll have the coordinates in forty-five minutes or less."

"Counting on you, brother," Cal said. "Charlie, out."

The line went dead as Lucas sucked in a breath of surprise.

"Are you okay?" Lilah asked. At the same time, Haven rose from sleep and put his head on his handler's shoulder.

"Wow," Lucas said with a shake of his head as he

pressed a fist to his chest. "That was the first time he called me brother instead of kid. I wasn't expecting it."

"I'm confused?"

Lucas reached back to stroke Haven's head while he processed the moment. Once he had, he turned to her with a smile. "The guys always called me son or kid, but it didn't bother me. I'm the youngest and the newest on the crew, so I accepted it as being under their wing and learning the ropes."

"Now you're equals."

He tipped his head in agreement as he put the van into Drive and let off the brake. "And I'm not going to let them, or you, down now."

"You won't let me down, Luca," she promised, squeezing his shoulder. "We're a team, but you're the leader. How do I help?"

"Watch our six," he answered, pulling onto the road again just as dawn finished breaking. "Let me know if we pick up company. I need to concentrate on finding a place to meet the team. One way or the other, this war ends today."

There was no greater feeling in the world than knowing he had found a brotherhood again, and that was what Cal had given him with one simple word. It was time to prove to the team that he'd earned it. Glancing at the woman beside him, with all her attention focused on the side mirror, made him wonder if they could be a team when this mission ended. The part of him who remembered their summer together said yes, but the other part of him, the part that needed Haven to live his life, reminded him that she deserved better than the life he could give her. He'd do well to remember that.

Chapter Twenty

The truth of the situation settled low in Delilah's belly when she lowered the binoculars. "There's not much for cover anywhere."

Cal grunted his agreement. "The forest on the western edge will help, but you still have to cross three acres to reach the garage from the woods, while the other three sides would remain unprotected."

When Luca found an abandoned gas station to use as a meeting place, they parked the van behind it and got busy gearing up while they waited for the rest of the team. Their first step was to check out the property, which they'd been doing for three hours, and there'd been no movement in or around it other than four-legged visitors. Unfortunately, their options were limited with their approach to the garage, something she suspected Burris had planned for.

"Anyone else wonder why he built a garage smack-dab in the middle of a field without easy accessibility?" Luca asked, lowering his binoculars, too.

"It crossed my mind," Cal agreed. "I'm starting to think we're barking up the wrong tree. If they're hiding price-less artifacts in that garage, there's no way to move them in and out without being seen. There's no power out here, so there can't be cameras or a security system unless it's solar powered."

"You could move them under the cover of darkness," Luca said, glancing up at the darkening sky as another snow shower approached. "Still not ideal for vehicle access or moving about unnoticed, though."

"Or it's the perfect situation," Lilah said slowly, bringing the binoculars back to her face. "All you need is a shotgun, boots and a camo jacket with an ATV parked outside the door. Not a soul pays attention to a hunter on their own land. Not in this part of the country."

"She's got a point," Roman agreed, setting his notebook down. "For right or wrong, we have to make a decision."

"We're going in," Delilah said without hesitation. "There's no choice. If we're correct, the auction will be in three days. We can't allow it to happen. If we can rule this place out, we know our next target is confronting Burris at home."

"Agreed," Luca said. She smiled, happy to have him on her side. "Chances are, it won't take long to clear the place, but if we're lucky, we find something that tells us where to go next. Cal, Roman, Lilah and I will go through the woods on the west side. Cal and Roman will hold coverage there while Lilah and I approach the building."

"What about the other three sides of the building?" Cal asked, a brow raised.

"Mack keeps mobile command secure and the communications running while Eric runs the drone overhead," Luca said. "Selina," he said, turning to the woman who had kept them all alive for years. "You and Efren take our van behind the property and find a place for him to set up his gun. You may have to trespass, but again, we have few options."

"We'll go through the forest on the west side and find a tree stand. Burris may not hunt, but I assure you, others do, so there's bound to be a few stands out there. That will give me a view from above that will cover the entire perimeter of the garage," Efren said, having thought it out already.

"Excellent," Lucas said with a thankful nod. "We'll give you a head start. If you see anything, alert Cal and Roman. It's not ideal, but again, we have few options in this situation."

"Agreed," Cal said with finality.

Selina and Efren were already getting their gear on. "We're heading out now. Give us twenty minutes of scout time, but we'll be on coms," Selina said, fitting one in her ear. "We'll let you know if we encounter anything that will change the current plan."

"Ten-four," Cal said as they exited the mobile command station and disappeared. He addressed Lucas again. "All of that said, you'll have to hold your own out there if someone approaches. We're easily—" he put the binoculars to his face and swung them back and forth between the woods and the garage "—five minutes out, and that's if we're not dodging bullets."

"Understood," Luca said. "I say we move soon. The snow will give us cover."

With everyone's jobs defined, they prepared their gear for the trip, including lights for Delilah's pistol and Luca's long gun. She didn't want to carry a rifle, fearing it would slow her down. Lucas was taller, stronger and better suited for carrying a gun that size through knee-deep snow. Besides, the garage was small, which made her think this was all a lesson in futility, but when it came to her life, she could leave no stone unturned.

"Ready?" she asked, checking that her pistol was easily accessible.

"I'm in the lead," Luca said, taking her hand and pulling her to the door where Haven waited. "I'll plow through the snow, and you follow in my footprints with Haven."

"We're on your rudder," Cal said as he and Roman lined up behind them.

With a nod, they exited mobile command and found their way into the woods. The walk would be long, but it was the only way to keep their vehicles away from Burris's land on the off chance it was being monitored, or he showed up.

Lucas moved quicker than expected, and she found it challenging to keep up with him, especially trying to keep clear of Haven. She bent over to catch her breath when they reached the forest's edge.

"I'm short, Luca," she said, puffing air from her lips. "Give me a second to catch up."

Luca hung back and waited for Cal and Roman to approach them. Once they were together, she stood, and Cal motioned to his right. "There's a thicker grouping of trees that will give us good cover about a hundred yards down. Give us a few to get set up before you head toward the garage. Tango and Sierra, are you in place?" He was addressing Efren and Selina now, as they'd been quiet throughout the walk.

"Ten-four," Efren whispered. "Just made it into a tree stand. Sierra is on the spotting scope. So far, it's still clear. Proceed with usual caution."

Cal nodded at them before he and Roman broke off and headed away. Luca clicked off their microphones before resting his forehead on hers. As the snow melted on her glasses, he shimmered before her like an angel come to save her. "No heroics, got it?"

"I don't see any reason why they'll be needed, but I'll say the same to you," she whispered. "I also want to say thank you. Thank you for stepping up and helping me when you didn't have to."

"Thank you for reminding me that I can do hard things."

She smiled then, her heart cracking open as he used her words in a way that held so much honesty and truth. "Let's do one more hard thing and find justice for our fallen soldiers. Right?"

"Right, but first..." He removed his glove and pulled a cloth from his pocket before gently removing her glasses. Carefully, he wiped them down with the cloth and slid them back on her face. "There's the pair of eyes I see in my dreams," he said with a wink before he stowed the cloth.

Her heart nearly melted into a pool of mush on the forest floor, knowing he had brought the cloth to keep her vision clear. Even with Cal's special coating applied to them, he knew the snow would be a problem for her. He still cared about her, which gave her hope that they could remain friends when this was over.

Once Luca was ready again, he grabbed her hand and pulled her to the edge of the trees. "On my lead." She nodded, and he took off, Haven tight by his side this time.

The closer she got to the building, the more fear and dread built in her belly. A garage in the middle of a field felt like hiding in plain sight, and she worried whatever they were hiding was going to get her killed.

Once they were through the open space, they stood tight to the side of the building and took a moment to catch their breath. Their earlier assessment had been correct. There were no cameras under the eave of the garage. There may not be power out here, but you could buy solar-powered camera units, so that was another red flag as far as she was concerned.

"I'm telling you, Lucas. Burris isn't dumb. There's no way he'd put anything here without cameras or more security. This is a futile endeavor."

"Maybe, but there may be something else in there that will help us sort this out. Old paperwork or equipment that we can jack the black box on," he answered. "Mina is still running down Burris's finances and doing another property search."

"I wish she could have gotten into that chat room," Lilah whispered. "If we knew who *Iamthatguy* and *Bigmanoncampus* are, then we'd know if we're on the right track." A little voice said she did know who they were. She just didn't want to admit it to herself.

"Unfortunately, that's lost to us for good, so all we can do is the legwork. Eventually, something will break. Keep your light off until we're inside and I've secured the door."

"Got it," she said, flipping her microphone back on as she crouched low and worked their way down the side of the garage.

Delilah stood behind Lucas while he inspected the side door, pulling his lock-picking kit from his vest. He glanced at her and checked the knob, a look of shock crossing his face when the door swung open. Haven was at his side as he swung his gun around the opening before stepping inside. Delilah followed from the rear and pushed the door closed.

"Door secure," she whispered, knowing the team could hear them, too. "Why wasn't it locked?" Before Lucas could answer, Haven growled low in his throat in a way she had never heard before. "What's wrong with him?"

"I don't know," Luca answered. "Haven, rest."

The dog didn't follow his handler's orders. Instead, he bolted to the right behind a pile of boxes.

"Haven. Return," Lucas hissed as he flicked on the gun's flashlight. She did the same with hers, illuminating a simple one-car garage filled with boxes.

"Do you smell the copper, too?" she asked, moving closer to where Haven had disappeared.

"Haven, return!" Luca said again as they walked around the boxes, but he stopped short. Lilah bumped into him before she could stop herself. "That explains the smell."

"What?" Cal asked through their earpiece. "Give me an update."

"Dead body," Lilah said, strangely detached. "Haven found him behind a pile of boxes."

"Him?"

"Definitely male," Luca said. "I haven't rolled him yet."

"There's no need," Lilah said, knowing who it was. "It's George Burris," she whispered, motioning at his left knee for Luca to see. "He had that knee brace made after he was hurt on a mission. He had to wear it all the time."

"Repeat. You've found Major George Burris dead?" Cal asked through their earpiece.

"Affirmative," Lilah said with her lips in a thin line.

"Looks like a round to the chest from the exit wound I can see on his back, as well as a round to his temple," Lucas reported.

"Where is his weapon?" Efren asked.

"Sidearm on his belt," Lilah answered.

"Rifle resting on a box five feet away," Lucas added. "Not staged as a suicide."

"He knew his attacker then and didn't feel threatened," Efren responded.

"You need to get out of there," Cal said. "I'm not ready to deal with the murder of an army major."

"We haven't had a chance to look around. Give us five?" Lilah asked.

"Negative. Get out while the snow is falling to cover your tracks. I do not want to deal with the police and the army."

"Not the army," Lilah said, motioning to Lucas to spread out and search. "He's been discharged, so he's a civilian now."

"All the same," Cal said, and she could picture him rolling his eyes. "We need to move out."

"No one wants to know why someone shot a former army major in his garage?" Efren asked, making Lilah snort internally. "Can you tell how long he's been down?"

"Not long. Maybe twelve hours," Lucas said. "Doubtful anyone would be worried yet."

Lilah was walking around the garage, which was big enough for a car or a boat but not much else. "These boxes are empty," she said, pushing on one until it fell to the ground. "There's nothing in this garage."

"Except for a dead army major and you two. Get out.

Now," Cal repeated, and they looked at each other, their brows raised.

"Ten-four," Luca said, shaking his head at Lilah and clicking his mic off. She did the same while he walked over to her. "We have two minutes. Go."

Lilah walked behind the boxes she dumped, shining her flashlight around the floor and the walls, looking for anything that shouldn't be there or didn't belong there, but the garage was filled with empty boxes and nothing else. Haven had his nose on the ground as he sniffed through the garage. His ears pointed to the ceiling as he went, and his concentration was undeterred by Luca's commands.

"Why didn't they pour a concrete pad for this building?" Lucas asked, bouncing on the floor a bit. "Plywood is going to rot in these conditions."

"It feels temporary to me," Lilah said, motioning at the walls that were nothing more than studs and particle board. "Like they had no intention of using it very long."

Haven growled again, the sound raising the hair on the back of her neck. "Luca, we need to get out of here. Haven is a mess."

Luca walked to his dog and crouched low. "Haven is a retired war dog, but he's acting like an active one now. He's reacting to the major's death."

Lilah walked up behind him, her boots thudding across the cheap plywood. It was her final step that made her pause. "Did you hear that?" She stepped back on her right foot just as there was a metallic snap. The floor bounced, and they jumped back, their eyes locking when the floor no longer sat flush.

"Trapdoor?" she mouthed to Luca, who nodded. He

motioned her to flip her mic back on as Cal demanded to know where they were.

"Secure one, Lima," he said, letting them know they were now in a situation that required rapt attention. "On our way out, Lilah tripped a trapdoor. Give us three to investigate it."

"Negative," Cal instructed. "Get out of there now. There's already one dead body in there. I don't want three."

"There's no one here, boss. I suspect whatever is below us is empty, but this is why we're here. It could be the answer we're looking for right below our feet."

They both heard Cal's heavy sigh on the other end of the mic. "Fine. Charlie and Romeo will approach."

"Affirmative," Luca said, flipping the mic off while motioning for Lilah to stand back. She stepped out of the way and grabbed the handle on Haven's vest to hold him back. She nodded, and he lifted the door, sweeping his gun across the opening. "Empty," he said, motioning for her to look down the hole. "Notice the stairs?"

"Well made." There were even handrails on each side of the staircase going down. "I was expecting a rung ladder."

"Me, too, but this tells a different story."

"A story of someone with a bad knee using them frequently?"

Luca nodded with his foot on the first step. "Haven, return." As soon as Lilah released the dog, he followed Lucas. They went down the stairs back-to-back so he could sweep the space on the way down as she kept her sidearm pointed at the top. It was possible Burris's killer might show up before Cal and Roman.

"These steps are better made than the floor above

them." He swung his flashlight around, assessing the situation. "Old shipping container," he said. "They must have buried it and built the garage above it."

Their feet hit the container floor and Lilah swung her flashlight along the wall, illuminating shelves that ran the entire length on both sides, all filled with relics of a different time and place.

"I believe it's time to call in the cavalry," she whispered, her heart sinking at the thought. Once again, her problem would become his and Secure One's by default, but it was too late to back out. All she could do was go forward and pray that of the two left who knew about these artifacts, she was the last one standing.

NONE OF THIS made sense. Lucas walked along the side of the wall in shock and horror to see so many treasures from other countries. "Someone has done all the provenance on these," Lilah said, pointing to documentation next to each treasure. "They're ready for an auction."

"That probably explains why Burris is upstairs dead," Lucas said, his gaze trained on two bronze chalices on a shelf. "Whoever he's working with double-crossed him." He stared at the cups on the shelf, willing his memory to recall where he'd seen them.

"Mack, we need to contact the local police, military police, homeland security and JAG. We must establish a chain of command and custody for these relics, not to mention, deal with the murder victim," he heard Lilah say. Still, his mind was off in a different time and place.

"Porter, let no one through these doors until we return."

"Yes, Colonel Swenson." He held the door for the

colonel and two other men that Swenson had simply introduced as "men of faith." Lucas could only assume they were local church leaders or priests who had information for the government, but that was above his pay grade. His job was to make sure the colonel didn't die on this social visit.

He climbed inside the Humvee and sat at the gun turret. He wasn't happy when he'd been assigned to take the colonel out alone, but Swenson had insisted they weren't in combat territory and the locals were their allies. Lucas didn't believe for a hot second that anyone in this hellhole of a country was their ally. He'd seen far too many of them blow up his friends. He trusted no one except his K-9, Hercules, who stood at attention by the door, his head swinging right and left as he scanned for enemies and listened for vehicles approaching.

As a munitions officer, it wasn't Lucas's job to be out using the ammunition. It was his job to make sure they had enough. He wasn't given a choice today when Colonel Swenson needed backup immediately and no one else was available.

"In and out, right, Hercules?" he asked the dog while they waited in the hot desert sun. Sweat dripped down his spine, running a shiver through him. Something was off. He swung the gun around, expecting an ambush, but finding nothing in any direction. "Come on," he hummed, glancing at the building door and praying it would open. His sixth sense was telling him to get out of there now. He pressed the button on his walkie-talkie. "Porter to Colonel Swenson. ETA?"

"Coming now," was the answer.

Lucas hopped down from the gun and opened the pas-

senger side door of the Humvee. He commanded Hercu-
les to stand next to him. Swenson was the first to emerge,
and then the two men, one carrying a large white bag.

Lucas didn't get a word out to the colonel before a
barrage of bullets struck the stucco wall behind them.
Lucas swung his gun around and sprayed the area, un-
sure where the enemy was. "Get in!" he yelled to the col-
onel, standing over the two men sprawled on the ground.
"Get in, now!"

Swenson grabbed the white bag and jumped in the
open passenger door. Hercules followed him in while
Lucas sent another burst of gunfire and then slid into
the driver's side. He threw it into gear and took off, sand
and gravel flying from under the tires.

"I thought the locals were our allies!" Lucas yelled,
angry that, once again, they'd been lied to. "Who were
those guys?"

"Men of faith," Swenson said again. "They're the
only two dead, which should tell you something."

"Why would anyone want men of faith dead?"

"I can't answer that, Porter. Just get us back to base
in one piece."

"Yes, sir," Lucas answered between clenched teeth.
He pretended not to notice the bag by the colonel's feet
that had fallen open and revealed a bronze chalice...

"Luca?" He turned his head as reality filtered back
in. Haven had his nose pressed hard into his thigh, so he
took a minute to breathe in threes, noting his heart rate
slowing as he stroked Haven's head. "Thanks, buddy.
I'm fine."

"You look like you saw a ghost," Lilah said, still
swinging her flashlight around the space. There were

dark corners he didn't like. He was praying Cal arrived soon with backup.

"I may have," he said, motioning at the chalices. "I've seen these before."

"What? Where?"

"I'd been on the base about two weeks when Colonel Swenson wanted transport with two other men to a building in a small village. Everyone else was busy, so he demanded I take him."

"Alone?"

He nodded. "I told him it wasn't a good idea, but he wasn't budging."

"Which meant you couldn't ignore a direct order."

"Not without spending time in the brig. Four of us went out, but two came back, along with these chalices. Do you remember putting these through for shipping?"

Lilah shook her head, her lips in a thin line. "I recognize only about half of these items, Luca. I'm starting to think those dead women were doing the same thing for him as I was, but on different bases."

"Only they weren't going to museums. My logical mind had Burris building a personal collection, but with him upstairs dead, I'm starting to think he was the grunt man for someone much higher up."

"That memory you had is the answer."

"Colonel Swenson?"

Before she could nod, clapping started from the darkness. Lucas swung around, bringing his gun to his shoulder as a man stepped into the beam of his flashlight. Lucas felt his world tip when the man before him was indeed Colonel Swenson. "Aren't you smart?" he asked as Lilah's flashlight illuminated the item they'd been searching for all this time. Behind Swenson was the trunk—half a tablet present in the top.

"Colonel Swenson?"

"That's Major General to you, Porter," he spat. "And you," he said, addressing Lilah. "You have been a trial. I have to say, I'm glad this is over." He kept his gun at his shoulder but stretched his back. "Thank goodness you finally arrived. Do you know how uncomfortable the floor is in a storage container?"

"You knew we were coming?"

"The alert that someone accessed the chat room told me it was time to take care of some final business. I always knew you had the file, but as long as you didn't click on it, I could keep you alive. Now, I'm afraid that's no longer possible. Especially since you know of my involvement in this. Since I couldn't track you—you finally caught on to the medal. Good job," he said with a sarcastic smirk. "I hedged my bets that you'd end up looking for Burris once you decided he had the answers. Sad, but you know what they say, dead men don't speak."

"Just tell me why," Lilah said, stepping closer to Lucas as Swenson advanced on them. "Tell me why I was tracked and harassed for so long."

"You were a real pain in my back quarter, Hartman. You were tracked because you had all the information in your head about these little baubles," he said, swinging his arm out at the wall. "Not to mention, you saw The Lost Key of Honor file. I had to keep you quiet until the auction."

Lilah whistled, and a shiver ran down Lucas's spine.

"It's a shame that I saved all the information about these—what did you call them?—baubles to a flash drive before the base fell," Lilah said, doing exactly that. "It's already in the hands of the authorities. It would have been smarter to kill me, but you didn't. You took great pleasure in slicing me up, but why play the game with me when you killed the other four women?"

Lucas tried not to react to the information that Swenson was The Mask. He wondered if Delilah knew who was behind it before they even set foot in this basement and never told him. Haven leaned in hard against his leg, a steady low growl coming from his throat as he glared at the man before him.

Swenson raked Lilah lasciviously. "I have to say, I always wondered what my creations looked like once they healed. Your chin," he said, motioning at her face. "Not bad work there. I do hope your gut healed well."

"You son of a—"

Lilah cut Lucas off. "You didn't answer my question. Why didn't you just kill me like you did the other women?"

"We were still looking for one more artifact. On the off chance I needed to have a little chat with you about something you may have seen or heard, you had to be breathing."

"The Lost Key of Honor," Lilah said as Swenson smiled like an animated horror puppet.

"Such a powerful name, right?" he asked, almost giddy as he advanced on them. "I'm sure you can understand why it was important to keep you out of the picture until I could ascertain the piece and finish the auction."

"And did you?" Lucas asked. "Ascertain the piece, that is."

Swenson's smile dissipated, and he shook his head.

"Unfortunately, no, but the auction will still happen. I have too many people looking for these trinkets, and I can't disappoint them on Christmas morning. I still have a few days to decide what to do with the trunk. Our time together is over, though. I do wish I had my knife and an unlimited amount of time to turn you into beautiful artwork, but I don't, so a bullet to the head for each of you will have to do."

There was commotion overhead, and then Cal yelled, "Secure One, drop your weapon!"

Cal and Roman came barreling down the stairs, and Haven pounced at Swenson. A gunshot rang out, and Lucas stumbled backward into Cal, who lowered him to the ground. Lilah fired three times in quick succession.

"Haven!" Lucas screamed, afraid the dog was in the line of fire. "Haven! Return!"

The small space quickly became chaotic as it filled with team members yelling different things simultaneously. Lucas sat there, detached from the room and his body as he breathed in to three, held it for three and let it out to three.

"Luca!" Lilah said, dropping the gun and running to him. "Call an ambulance!" she yelled as Lucas watched Cal handcuff a raving Swenson. Lilah's bullets had found a home in his shoulder, arm and knee. None of them were life-threatening, but satisfying nonetheless to inflict a little pain on someone who had tortured her for years.

"You're going to be okay," she said, but the expression on her face said something else entirely. She stripped off her jacket and held it to his chest, pushing so hard it made him grunt with pain. "I know. I'm sorry to hurt you, but I need to keep pressure on this wound."

"Wound?" he asked, his voice holding disbelief.

"Swenson shot you," she explained. "If Haven hadn't pounced on his arm at the last second, the bullet would be in your head. You'd be dead."

"That rhymes," he said, laughing once before he started to cough, the taste of blood in his mouth.

"Don't talk, just conserve your energy," she ordered, so close he could kiss her.

"Don't leave me, Delilah Porter," he whispered, his words stuttering as he spoke. "I will follow you anywhere."

She brushed the hair back off his forehead and kissed him. "All the days since I left you, I've wished my name was Delilah Porter," she whispered. "I'm not going anywhere. Everything I've done for the last six years has been for you. To protect you. To keep you safe, but in the end, I couldn't do that. You can't die on me now, do you understand? You have to hang on. Hang on, Luca."

It wasn't lost on him that he had this woman back in his life because death came calling and he'd answered the phone. He'd been given the gift of a little more time, something others often weren't fortunate enough to get, and he hadn't wasted a moment of it. Lucas had brought closure to a situation he never thought he would, and for that, he was grateful. If death took him this time, he would accept that his work here was done. Then she pressed her lips to his, and he knew he'd die a very happy man.

Chapter Twenty-One

The old adage that no good deed goes unpunished had settled deep in Delilah's bones as soon as the military and homeland security arrived at the shipping container. The man she loved was hauled away by ambulance while she was forced into custody as a party to real war crimes. While she'd been treated well and was comfortable, she'd spent the last two days under lock and key while they tried to sort out who knew what in this bizarre case of unabashed greed.

Thankfully, she could use the flash drive and screenshots of the chat room to her advantage. It turned out that *Iamthatguy* was Burris and *Bigmanoncampus* was Swenson. She should have thought of that sooner, but honestly, she didn't have officers of the US Army stealing antiquities to sell on the black market on her bingo card. That was what they had planned to do, though.

The way Swenson told it, they started with good intentions, wanting to help the locals, but they quickly realized what the relics were worth on the black market and how easy it was to make them disappear. Sadly, the one thing she wasn't expecting was to learn that the base was attacked because of Swenson's and Burris's actions.

They had systematically gone out and killed every person who had turned in relics to the base. It was easy to make it look like they died in the war, but if there was no one left who knew where the relics went, there was no one to thwart their plan. No one but her, that is. The locals didn't believe that revenge was best served cold. They believed in immediate revenge in the most brutal of ways. A shudder went through her at the memory.

"Are you cold? I can turn the heat up," Mina said.

"No, I'm fine," she answered, staring out the window at the white fields stretching as far as the eye could see. "I was just thinking about what Swenson told the police. Evil on a level I never want to see again, Mina. How could I be so wrong about them? How did I not see the evil?"

"The true psychopaths in our midst never reveal themselves, Delilah. We've seen it so many times. Look at my situation with the FBI. No one would have seen that coming."

"True," she whispered, staring at her hands as they drove silently for a few miles. "The army offered me veteran benefits."

Mina lifted a brow as she steered the van around a curve. "Disability benefits?"

"Yep, as well as the Secretary of the Army Award for Valor along with the Purple Heart, neither of which I want."

"The Purple Heart is for those wounded in battle during active duty."

"True, but PTSD and a traumatic brain injury may not be visible but still qualify. Also, these are quite visible," she said, motioning at her chin. "The stabbings weren't while I was on active duty, but from what I understand, it came down from rather high up on the chain of command. The other four women will also be receiving them posthumously. I want to refuse them both."

"Unfortunately, that's not how it works, Delilah," Mina said with a chuckle. "When you're the pivotal person to help return priceless artwork and antiques to their respective home countries and paid heavily because of it, you get medals."

"And a whole lot of memories I'd rather not have."

"Now, that's a true story." She nodded. "Cal told us they offered you a job."

"Ha! Yeah, like I'm going to go back to work for the government. Hard pass."

Mina's lips tipped up. "Can't say that I blame you there. You've been through enough."

"How bad was it for Cal, Mina?"

"Secure One came out just fine, so don't worry. Don't forget that Cal is an army veteran. He was looking out for another, and we had plenty of paperwork to prove it. We were out of there within a day. I wish the same had been true for you."

"Me, too. I want to see Luca. How is he? I talked to him yesterday and he said he was feeling fine, but he hasn't responded to my text from this morning."

"He's only alive because Haven pounced on Swenson. He was using armor-piercing rounds in that gun. Lucas would be dead."

"I'm not sure a bullet to the chest is much better, but I'm glad that he's healing." She sighed, and it was heavily weighted with sadness. "When we talk now, it's awkward because I don't know what to say to the man who saved my life. I can't face him knowing he took two bullets for me in the span of a week."

Mina's laughter filled the van as she turned right and guided them down a narrow road. "Sweetheart, that man would take all the bullets for you. You'll know the right things to say when you see him again. Just trust your heart."

Sure, trust your heart, she says. That's hard to do when you aren't sure if it'll get stomped on. Would Luca stomp on her heart intentionally? No, but she was afraid of the unintentional consequences of this event, especially since she had no one else in her life but him and the team at Secure One.

When Delilah glanced out the car window, she was surprised. "Why are we at a cemetery? You said I had to talk to the Rochester Police about the incident."

"You do, but someone else will be taking you there. I'm officially off duty."

She barely heard a word Mina said as she stared through the windshield, the sun making it hard to see anything, but she did notice a man standing in front of a grave with a dog at his side. "Luca?"

"Go to him. You need each other right now."

"But, Mina, what do I say?" Her question was desperate as she turned to the woman she had come to count on as a friend and confidant.

"The truth." Mina reached into the back of the van and grabbed Delilah's winter coat, which she shrugged on, along with a hat, scarf and gloves.

Was she prolonging the inevitable? Maybe, but knowing it was time to face the man she had loved for six long years made her pause and search her heart for the words she'd need when she faced him again. She slung her purse around her shoulder and let out a sigh.

"Thanks for the ride and the advice, Mina. Merry Christmas," she said, throwing her arms around her friend. "Be careful on the drive home."

"Roman is waiting at the police station. I'll pick him up and head home while you ride with Lucas and Haven."

With a nod, Delilah pushed the van door open and climbed out, her eyes glued to the man just a few feet in front of her, his back turned as he stared at a gravestone.

"Hey, there, Lilah," he said, his back still to her.

"Luca," she said, but blinked twice when she realized he was wearing his dress uniform, his polished black shoes reflecting the sunlight as she glanced down at the grave marker. It read Tamara Porter. "Your mom's grave?"

"I thought since I was down here, I'd let her see me in my dress uniform on Christmas morning. Better late than never, right?"

Her heart wanted to burst at the implications of this moment. "Luca, I'm stunned."

"You shouldn't be. You were right, Lilah. I gave that bag way too much power, and it was time I stopped. It's time to change the way I think about what I did in the service, and that's already helped with my anxiety. You reminded me to stop feeling guilty about who I lost by remembering who I saved. It's still a work in progress, but now I wake up with less burden from the past and more hope for the future."

"I'm happy for you, Luca," she said, leaning into him. "Are you okay? I need to know that you aren't in pain."

He took her hand and brought it to his chest, pushing it against his skin. He didn't flinch. "No pain. It was a through and through, so a few stitches and a few weeks means it will be nothing more than a scar. We all have them, right?"

"Some of us more than others." That was when she saw it. "Luca," she whispered, glancing up at him. "Your medals." She ran her hand across the row of medals now attached to his uniform.

He shrugged but avoided her gaze. "If there was one thing my mother was proud of me for, it was my service. I wore them for her this morning."

"She was a proud army mom," she agreed with a smile. "Nice touch. I know wherever she is over the rainbow, she's never been prouder."

"One down then," he said, finally turning to her and taking her hands.

"One down then?" she asked, confusion filling her voice. "I don't understand."

"Being here in this uniform is a reminder that one woman I love is proud of me. Now I need to know if the other woman I love is proud of me, too."

"Me?" Delilah asked, and he nodded, smiling as she nearly melted into the snow with relief.

"I've loved you since the moment I picked you up off that tarmac, Delilah Hartman. I told myself that day I was going to marry you. I intend to keep that promise or die trying."

"You've nearly died trying enough times, Lucas Porter!" she exclaimed, watching a smile grow on his face. "You don't need to keep trying. I love you, Luca, and I'm overwhelmingly proud of what you've overcome to be standing in this uniform today. I sent you to that clinic alone six years ago because I loved you. I walked away from you that day and stayed away for the same reason. I would do anything to protect and keep you safe, even if it meant we could never be together."

"That's over now, my darling Delilah," he promised, lowering his head for a kiss that warmed her head to toe even on this cold Christmas morning. When he lifted his head, his eyes glowed with happiness in a way she had never seen. "I want to explore us," he said, holding her tightly. "I don't know how that will work since we live such different lives, but I know one thing. I'll follow you anywhere. I know you got a job offer from the army. If you want to take it, say the word. I'll be right behind you—"

Delilah put her finger to his lips. "Secure one, Delta."

Her smile grew when his brows went up. "What now?"

"Turns out, another job offer awaited me in the civilian sector. Cal offered me a position as a cybersecurity tech to work with Mina, building Secure Watch, the new division for Secure One. I accepted this morning. I want to be with you, Luca, through the good times and the bad. I know that sometimes our memories paint outside the lines of the present, but we'll face those together, too. How do you feel about that?" Her question held a tinge of nervousness as she waited for his answer.

"I think there's only one thing left to say, Delilah Hartman."

"Then say it, Lucas Porter."

"Secure two, Lima."

Then his lips were back on hers as they stood in the bright sunshine of a day that, for the first time in years, offered her true joy, hope and peace. They shared the first kiss of the rest of their lives, ready to focus on a future they could build together from a place of love, understanding and acceptance of their past that led them to this place in time. His tender kiss was a layer of comfort over the jagged scars in her soul, assuring her that he'd heal them completely with enough time.

"Happy?" he asked, lifting his lips from hers.

"Better than happy," she whispered.

"What's better than happy?"

"Being healed."

A smile lifted his lips as they neared hers again. "I couldn't agree more. Merry Christmas, my darling Delilah," he said, pulling her steamed-up glasses from her face.

"Merry Christmas, Luca," she whispered before they shared another kiss to the sound of Haven's joyful barking.

* * * * *

If you missed the previous books in Katie Mettner's Secure One miniseries, they're available now wherever Harlequin Intrigue books are sold:

Going Rogue in Red Rye County
The Perfect Witness
The Red River Slayer
The Silent Setup
The Masquerading Twin

HARLEQUIN
Reader Service

Enjoyed your book?

Try the perfect subscription for Romance readers and get more great books like this delivered right to your door.

See why over 10+ million readers have tried Harlequin Reader Service.

Start with a Free Welcome Collection with free books and a gift—valued over $20.

Choose any series in print or ebook.
See website for details and order today:

TryReaderService.com/subscriptions